BEACH BLANKET SANTA

By
Ginny Baird

Published by
Winter Wedding Press

Copyright 2013
Ginny Baird
Trade Paperback
ISBN 978-0-9886953-2-0

All Rights Reserved
No portions of this work may be reproduced
without express permission of the author.
Characters in this book are fiction and figments of
the author's imagination.

Edited by Linda Ingmanson
Cover by Dar Albert

About the Author

From the time that she could talk, romance author Ginny Baird was making up stories, much to the delight -- and consternation -- of her family and friends. By grade school, she'd turned that inclination into a talent, whereby her teacher allowed her to write and produce plays, rather than write boring book reports. Ginny continued writing throughout college, where she contributed articles to her literary campus weekly, then later pursued a career managing international projects with the US State Department.

Ginny's held an assortment of jobs, including school teacher, freelance fashion model, and greeting card writer, and has published more than ten works of fiction and optioned nine screenplays. She's additionally published short stories, nonfiction and poetry, and admits to being a true romantic at heart.

Ginny is the author of several bestselling romantic comedies, including novellas in her *Holiday Brides Series*. She's a member of Romance Writers of America (RWA), the RWA Published Authors Network (PAN), and the RWA Published Authors Special Interest Chapter (PASIC).

When she's not writing, Ginny enjoys cooking, biking and spending time with her family in Tidewater, Virginia. She loves hearing from her readers by email at GinnyBairdRomance@gmail.com and welcome visitors to her website at http://www.ginnybairdromance.com.

Chapter One

"You know what you need?"

Matt Salvatore stared into his brother's deep blue eyes. They looked so much alike, people sometimes mistook them for twins. In fact, Robert was two years older and an inch shorter than Matt. Why then, did Matt get the feeling he wasn't measuring up? "No, but I suppose you're going to tell me."

Robert pushed back in his leather chair. They shared a lot of things between them, like a law practice in DC and the same dark hair and broad shoulders. From the frown on Robert's face, he was growing weary of bearing Matt's weight. "You need some time away, man. A break from this scene."

"How's that supposed to make things better?"

"Every girl you see reminds you of her. If she's blonde, she looks just like Katya. If she's a brunette, she looks just like Katya might have been had she decided to dye her—"

Matt flagged a palm at his brother. "Slow down there, pal. A man is dying, and all you can do is dance on his grave."

"I'm not dancing. I'm trying to help!"

"By bringing up Katya at every turn?"

Robert sighed. "It's been six months, buddy. She left you before your birthday in June."

"Yeah, and that was awesome, wasn't it?"

"It was…less than nice." His lips twisted in a wry smile. "Never can trust those Russians."

"She was a foreign correspondent. Not a spy."

"Seemed to slip in and out of those shadows pretty easily."

Matt ran a hand through his short, wavy hair, knowing Robert was right. Katya had been nothing if not slippery—with the truth more than anything else. She'd spent countless nights chasing after hot stories in Washington. It was only by mistake that Matt had learned of her questionable research tactics.

"What was that last guy's name? Carl Benton? Wasn't he running for Congress or something?"

"He lost."

"Well, at least that's some consolation." He leaned forward across his mahogany desk. "Bro, I've got to tell you, I'm starting to worry. This Katya thing has got you all eaten up. And for what? She's just not worth it."

"I apologize if I haven't been at the top of my game."

Robert lifted his brow.

"But things will get better. I swear. I'll turn this ship around."

"Sure you will." Robert's face brightened. "All you need is a little shore leave."

"Where's this going?"

Robert massaged his square jaw and studied him. "Straight to the Outer Banks, I hope."

"Your beach house?"

"You didn't graduate magna cum laude for nothing."

"What about it?"

"I think you should go there, take a breather."

"Who goes to the beach in December?"

"Nobody. That's what's great. You'll have no one to bring down with your sour mood."

"Thanks."

Robert laughed good-naturedly. "You know what I'm saying. It'll be good to have some time away. Read some of those dirty spy novels you're so crazy about."

"What is it with the espionage?"

"Okay, okay. Cast your reel out, then. Whatever floats your boat. Just get your tail out of Dodge for a while. It'll do you good."

Matt understood his brother was trying to help, but everyone knew depression loomed large around the holidays. With him already feeling down, was being even more alone really the answer? "You want me to spend Christmas by myself?"

Robert's expression softened. "That's not what I meant at all. I just want you to go regroup for a week, then join us in Maryland. Margaret and I want you to spend Christmas and New Year's with us."

"And your new baby," Matt reminded him.

"Well, yeah. Sure. Why not?"

Because babies screamed all night, as far as Matt recalled. They also needed diaper changing. This was sounding less and less like the dream bachelor vacation. "That's really good of you," Matt said, standing. "But I've already made plans."

Robert pinned him in place with his gaze. "Name them."

"Well, I was thinking of…" Suddenly it dawned on him that he didn't need to make excuses. Matt couldn't go to the beach. Christmas was always Elaine's week there. Elaine was Robert's first wife, and the one asset neither could bear to liquidate had been their beach house. Besides, with the real estate market having tanked, their oceanfront property was practically under water. So they'd opted to keep it awhile, carefully orchestrating a calendar of his-and-hers usage dates, so both could enjoy it without having to run into each other. "I thought Elaine always took Christmas week?"

"Usually, she does. But this year, she's getting married. Remember? She'll be on her honeymoon. The place is all yours!"

Matt started to think about that. The gentle melancholy of the seashore… A few six-packs of beer. Surf fishing in the waves. Letting his beard stubble grow for a week. Skipping out on the suit and tie routine… And finally—*finally*—forgetting about Katya. After a full week of that, he'd probably feel fine handling Christmas at the beach solo. Or, even heading back to Maryland if that was what he decided to do. Neither he nor Robert were going to Chicago this year. They and their siblings had pooled together to send his folks on a forty-year-anniversary trip to Tuscany's lake region. It would be one of the first seasons in memory the greater Salvatore clan hadn't gathered together to ring in the New Year, a plethora of grandchildren bustling about and blowing plastic horns. Of course, everyone had agreed it was worth it. There'd been tears in his mom's eyes at Thanksgiving when Robert, as the eldest, had handed over the airline tickets and broken the news. Everyone deserved the kind of happiness their parents shared. They'd stuck together through all kinds of weather and seemed to care for each other even more now than Matt had recalled as a kid.

"What about the Barnes case?" he asked his brother.

"I've put our team of interns on it. They'll be busy pulling documentation together until after the first." He shot Matt an encouraging grin. "There's really not much left for you to do here…other than pout."

"Hey!" Matt didn't pout. Did he? Scowl a little, perhaps. Take on the brooding look of an artist. Appear mysteriously morose... But pout? Not on your life he didn't. If this was what Katya had reduced him to, it was way past time to change it. So, yeah, maybe he'd been deluded into believing she was the love of his life. What with that sexy accent and sharp wit, she'd had him practically from hello. But now she was gone. Long gone, and it was time he stopped rehashing the past. It was ironic that the one woman he'd really fallen for had been the one to walk out on him. While Matt had never purposely hurt anybody, he did have a history of the being the *guy who was good with good-byes.* He'd become really adept at sensing when a woman was getting in deep and knew it was kinder to cut things off early rather than unfairly lead somebody on. Matt wasn't sure what he was looking for, but he believed he would know it when he saw it. With Katya, he'd just been vision impaired. Not that he'd ever let *that* happen again. "Give me that key."

Robert blinked in surprise. "Just like that? You're leaving already?"

Matt held out his hand, and Robert slid open his desk drawer, extracting a key chain with a dangling fake sand dollar attached. "Merry Christmas, brother," he said, slapping it into Matt's palm.

"Thanks. And Happy New Year to you."

"Wait a minute. You're not coming back to...?"

"I'll call you," Matt said with a wink.

Robert eyed him suspiciously. "You got another girl stashed away somewhere I don't know about? Someone you're taking there with you?"

"You wish," Matt said. *I wish*, he thought. But this year, he'd have no such luck. Matt had grown weary of the dating game. That fiasco with Katya had been the final blow. He'd already taken her home to meet the family. His big Italian family, grandmother and all. And she'd apparently bedded the congressional hopeful less than a week later. Matt was supposed to be smart, primed to see things. His work as a corporate attorney demanded keen mental acumen. But every single bit of his brainpower had let him down when Katya had batted her pretty green eyes. *Well, no more of that,* Matt thought, clutching the key. He was done with women for the next little bit. After this breather at the beach, he'd return refreshed to focus on his career. Robert really had been doing more than his share lately. And with a new baby at home, it simply wasn't fair. By all accounts, Matt was the one who should be picking up any extra slack. And he planned to see to it post haste.

Sarah Anderson refilled Elaine's slender sherry glass, then lightly fluffed her veil. "You look gorgeous," she said. "Really you do."

Elaine studied her reflection in the mirror. Her blonde hair was in a perfect updo with loose tendrils spilling forth. Though they were best friends, they couldn't have looked any more different. Sarah's curly brown hair spilled past her shoulders, its color matching her eyes. "I'm going to look gorgeous and drunk if you pour me another glass." Elaine took a sip and giggled.

Sarah adjusted the wedding gown at the shoulders and smiled. "You'll do just fine."

Elaine surveyed her maid of honor in the mirror. "Not drinking today, are we?"

Sarah caught her breath, recalling the last time she'd indulged at one of Elaine's weddings. "I think it's safer this way."

"Well, I wouldn't worry," Elaine said. "The groomsmen here aren't nearly as dishy as the first time around."

"Elaine! You're talking about Richard's brothers!"

"Oh, come on, Sarah. I may be engaged, but I still have eyes. Charlie and Hank are hot enough, but neither one is eye candy like—"

Sarah felt her cheeks flame. "Please don't remind me." It was all Sarah could do to forget waking up in the gorgeous Matt Salvatore's arms. He'd been the best man, and she the maid of honor. After one too many glasses of champagne and a lot of incredibly sexy slow dancing, they'd somehow wound up back at her place after the reception. She'd had a secret crush on Matt ever since first laying eyes on him at one of Elaine's pre-wedding parties. And when he'd kissed her on the dance floor, her knees had melted like butter. Sarah had never had a man kiss her that way. No one before, and nobody since.

"Those Salvatore men are pretty hard to resist," Elaine said with a knowing look.

"You divorced one of them."

"It's true. But it was for the best. Just look at how things have worked out. Robert met Margaret, and I've found"—she sighed longingly—"Hank."

Sarah took away her sherry. "Richard. You mean, Richard."

"That's right!" she said brightly.

Uh-oh, Sarah thought, wondering if maybe she'd poured one too many glass for the bride.

Someone knocked on the dressing room door. It was Janet, Richard's younger sister. "They want us upstairs in ten!"

Elaine hiccupped.

"Thanks, Janet," Sarah called, reaching for the water on the dresser. She gave Elaine the glass, urging her to take a long swallow. This sherry-drinking-before-the-wedding thing had been a tradition with their circle of girlfriends ever since Elaine's first time at it three years before. They'd all opened two bottles about an hour ago and toasted to Elaine's newfound happiness with Richard. While the other girls finished getting ready in the next room, Elaine had requested some time alone with her maid of honor.

Elaine drained the glass, then met Sarah's eyes. "Can I ask you something?"

"Anything. Ask."

"Do you find it perverse I only fall in love with R guys?"

"R guys?"

"Richard, Robert, Rodney, Rafael… What do you think it means?"

"I think you're thinking too much about it. It's a coincidence."

"Hmm." Elaine reached for the sherry bottle, but Sarah stopped her.

"They're almost ready for us upstairs."

"Right!" Elaine straightened herself on her stool. "Which is why I need you to make a promise."

Sarah pursed her lips a moment, eying her friend. "What kind of promise?"

"Come on, Sarah. Just say that you'll promise! It's my wedding day, okay?"

"Okay, okay. I promise."

Elaine beamed. "That a girl."

"What-a-girl?"

"You've just agreed to catch my bouquet!"

Sarah swallowed hard. The last thing she needed to do right now was go catching anybody's bouquet. Especially Elaine's. Given Elaine's wedding was today, that would put Sarah in line to marry next. Like that was destined to happen. Of course, that was just a silly superstition.

Elaine shot her a stern look. "You can't drop it. That would be bad luck."

"Maybe one of the other girls will elbow in," Sarah added hopefully. "Jennifer's been trying to nail down Louis for a while."

"Forget about Jennifer and Louis. I'm talking about you!"

"But I don't even have a boyfriend."

"No, Sarah. You don't. You never have a boyfriend, because when a guy asks you on a third date, you always run away."

"That's not true."

"What *is it* about that third date?"

Elaine picked up the sherry, despite Sarah's effort to stop her, and drank anyway. "Oh, I get it." She nodded in slow understanding, studying Sarah in the mirror. "That's like...getting-physical time, huh? You're afraid."

"I most certainly am not afraid," Sarah said, affronted. "I can...party with the best of them."

"I wasn't talking party. I was talking dancing." She wiggled her eyebrows. "Dirty dancing. You know, the two-to-tango kind. Lovers between the covers?"

A picture of her and Matt under the huge down comforter flashed through her mind. She flushed, pushing the murky memory aside.

"You have too much honeymoon on your mind," she told Elaine.

Elaine set down her glass, misty-eyed. "Yeah, maybe I do. Richard is *such* a tiger in the sack."

"Okay, up with you!" Sarah said, taking her friend by the elbow. "It's almost time to march."

"Ooh, I love this part, don't you?"

"It's special," Sarah said with a warm smile.

Elaine pulled her into her arms, and crinoline crunched. "You're special." She stifled a sob. "You've always been here for me. You're such a good friend."

Sarah patted her back. "I love you too."

"I wish I could give you something for Christmas."

"You have. That beautiful bracelet."

Elaine pulled back from their embrace. "I gave one of those to all the girls. And you're my maid of honor. I should have done something more."

"Just being here with you is enough."

"No, it's not. What do you want?"

"Want?"

"Go on. Name it."

"Elaine, you're getting married in eight minutes, I don't think now is the—"

"How about a vacation?" Elaine asked suddenly.

"What do you mean?"

"You love the beach."

"Like Hawaii?"

"That's a little hard to arrange last minute."

"I wasn't asking you to!"

Elaine's face became alive with excitement. "Bring me my purse," she said, pointing across the room.

Sarah crossed to the small love seat that held it and returned with it to Elaine, perplexed.

Elaine opened its clasp and extracted her key ring.

"What are you doing?" Sarah asked.

"Giving you my beach house," Elaine said with a grin. "For the week."

Sarah loved the beach and adored Elaine's cozy oceanfront cottage, but she couldn't possibly accept it so last minute. She had family to see in Bethesda and other arrangements to take care of besides. "Oh, Elaine, that's lovely, but—"

Elaine removed one key from her ring, the one with the dangling fake sand dollar hanging on a chain. "You simply can't refuse a gift from the bride. Especially on her wedding day."

Sarah thought of long walks on the beach…warm nights of reading by the fire… Elaine's cottage was the perfect getaway. And after the hubbub involved in helping arrange this massive wedding, a peaceful retreat sounded good. Better than good, almost like heaven.

"You don't have to stay there for Christmas, silly. Just use it as long as you'd like. It's my week, anyway. Otherwise it will go to waste."

Four hours later, Sarah saw the bridal bouquet hurtling in her direction like a rocket. Only this rocket had tiny jingling bells attached to its beautiful bright red ribbon. It had actually been Sarah's idea to add this extra holiday touch to the already festive candlelit wedding. It was one week before Christmas, and the entire church had been bedecked in lush greenery, boughs of holly draped from the arm of every pew. Sarah met Elaine's eyes in a panic as the flowers careened toward her. This was really happening. Elaine hadn't even bothered with the pretense of tossing the thing over her shoulder. She'd just grinned and lobbed it straight at Sarah.

Sarah swallowed hard as the musical menace closed in. Elaine's earlier words rang in her ears. *"You can't drop it. That would be bad luck"*. Sarah caught a glimpse of Jennifer standing in the wings and a sea of waving female arms outstretched. It was nearer now, just overhead and arching toward her. No! It was nose-diving to the floor! She had a split second to react and avert catastrophe. Sarah leapt skyward, and the weight of the flowers settled in her hands. There was a collective sigh from the guests, and then, after a split second of silence, a loud round of applause.

Sarah's cheeks burned. How she hated being the center of attention, particularly at moments like this. It was common knowledge she wasn't seeing anyone, and folks would wonder why she'd stolen the stage from Jennifer.

Louis surprised her with his approach and jovially patted her arm. "Nice catch," he said under his breath. Across the room, Jennifer narrowed her gaze and walked away. Sarah couldn't have felt any more awkward.

Then Elaine drew near with a stealthy thumbs-up. "I knew you wouldn't let me down."

Sarah lifted white roses to her nose, inhaling their sweet scent. "Why did you make me do that?" she asked in a whisper, disguised by the fanning bouquet.

"Because, hon. I want you to be as happy as I am. And, after a while"—she nudged the bouquet still clasped in Sarah's hands—"the right guy will come along. You'll see."

"Sure," Sarah said, not believing it. She was thirty-one-years old and hadn't met anyone with marriage potential yet. Not that it bothered her most days. She kept plenty busy with her work as an interior designer and truly loved what she did. It was hard to look for a mate in her field, which wasn't populated with many eligible men. And because Sarah wasn't into the bar or singles scene, she wasn't expressly searching anyhow. Who knew if the right guy for her was even out there? Even if he was, history had taught her that he'd be awfully hard to find.

"There's someone for everyone," Elaine said, smiling sweetly. "And somewhere out there is the perfect guy for you. You've just got to walk through the right door."

Chapter Two

Sarah let herself into Elaine's beach house and called out loudly, "Hello? *Hello?* Is somebody in here?" There was nothing but silence in return. Not that this surprised her. Renters at the cottage next door perpetually parked in Elaine and Robert's drive. She had to admit the landscape was confusing. You had to nearly be a native here to discern the obscure gravel road overgrown with sea ferns that included the neighboring cottage's drive. No matter. She'd stop by later and politely ask the renters to move their car. At the moment, neither was blocking the other in, so there was no real emergency.

Sarah set her suitcases in the kitchen and looked around the bright open space. Sporadic sunlight poured through the sliding glass doors adjoining a broad inviting deck beyond the living area. One side of the room held a rugged pine dining table with a matching bench and chairs. The other had a cozy stone fireplace surrounded by a large, comfy sofa, teak coffee table, and two reading chairs. A fire had been laid in the hearth with extra wood and kindling sticks stacked in a holder nearby. Although, it was hard to imagine building a fire on a day like today. The weather was unseasonably warm, in the sixties with partly cloudy skies and a mixture of light and dark clouds dotting the horizon. She'd heard a hard rain was coming and even that the weather might get dicey for a couple of days. But she'd brought enough supplies to last her, and for now, the beach appeared inviting enough. Sarah smiled as the ocean beyond the plate-glass windows heaved and sighed, white-tipped waves crashing onto an empty stretch of sand. As soon as she brought in her groceries, she'd kick off her shoes and go for a walk.

Down below the house and tucked in a corner behind the storage room, Matt finished his outdoor shower. Since the weather was predicated to change later with a cold front moving in, he'd decided to take advantage of bathing outside while he could. It might prove a tad chilly for some folks, who weren't as toughened to the elements as he was. But Matt, who'd engaged in rugged camping trips since he was a teen near Chicago, was well accustomed to some bite in the air. Compared to the Midwest in December, being in southern North Carolina felt almost like summertime.

There was something very freeing about being *au natural* outdoors, just a rustic wooden barrier between him and the path over the dunes. He'd had quite a catch today. Ten bluefish and nearly a dozen mackerel. Matt scrubbed his hands with extra care using the fisherman's soap he'd brought along to expunge any scent from the cleaning he'd done while still on the beach. He found it easier to take care of the messy work as soon as the need arose and had a simple fisherman's knife that had served him well for years. Matt planned to eat some of his haul while he was here, but most of it he planned to freeze and take back home. There were lots of recipes he could concoct, including a mighty delicious homemade gumbo.

Matt shut off the water, thinking he'd heard a car door slam shut. But that didn't make any sense. Not unless the cottage next door was rented for Christmas, which would be unusual since the house didn't even have a fireplace. And a fireplace at the beach in winter was something renters insisted on, no matter the weather. Matt squinted up at the sun lowering itself behind the dunes and grabbed his towel off a nearby hook. He'd head upstairs, freezer-bag the fish, and pop himself a brewski. *Yessirree*, he thought, winding the towel around his waist and cinching it. He was feeling better already. He hadn't thought about women all day.

Matt hoisted his heavy cooler in one hand while gripping his fishing tackle in the other. He'd just climbed the third wooden step to the side door when a screen door creaked open. Matt stopped in his tracks, thinking he'd heard footsteps. The next thing he knew, some pretty brunette was bounding down the stairs. She stared at him and fell back in fright.

"Oh!" she cried, dropping the flip-flops in her hand. One somersaulted down the steps, landing on Matt's bare foot. He quickly set down his stuff to grip the towel that was sliding south.

"Uh, hello," he said, securing the towel around him.

She stared at his waist, then quickly met his gaze. Matt caught his breath. He'd know those eyes anywhere. "Sarah?"

Her cheeks colored brightly as she swallowed hard. "Matt?" she asked with a squeak. "What are you doing here?"

He picked up her flip-flops and handed them to her, taking care with his towel the whole time. She wore snug jeans rolled up at the ankles and a fitted long-sleeve T-shirt. She was every bit as pretty as she'd been three years ago. Somehow, she looked even better. "Robert gave me the house for the week."

"Robert? But this is Elaine's week, isn't it?"

"Yes, but she's supposed to be on her honeymoon."

"She is."

"Then how…?"

"Elaine gave me the house for the week too. She said nobody would be using it."

Matt had worked hard to push memories of Sarah out his mind, but they all came flooding back now. She'd been so much fun at Elaine and Robert's wedding. He thought they'd really hit it off. Maybe even could start something. But then when the next morning came, she'd pushed him away. Naturally, he got over it. Matt knew better than to knock on doors where he wasn't wanted. And he'd met Katya shortly afterward besides. Matt felt a pang in his chest when the raw truth hit. Katya wasn't the first woman to let him down. It had really started with Sarah. "Then we're in a predicament, aren't we?"

"Well, yes. No," she said, backing up a step. "I should be the one to go. After all, you got here first."

"I don't see how that's fair. This really *is* Elaine's week, not Robert's."

He stared at her, and she stared back, her head and heart still grappling with the situation. Of all people to run into! *Matt Salvatore* with those unnerving blue eyes and that to-die-for statue-of-David body. It was bad enough that he had it; far worse that it was on such vivid display. The winds kicked up with a whistle, riffling his towel.

"If you don't mind," he said, lifting an eyebrow, "I think we should continue this conversation inside. It's getting a bit breezy out here."

"Of course," she said, quickly turning away and heading upstairs. She held the screen door open so he could make his way through with his collected gear. It was all she could do to avert her eyes from his solidly muscled shoulders and stop herself from thinking about what might have been. He hadn't changed at all. In some ways, he'd seemed to age in a way that made him appear even more handsome. And it was hard to top what he'd been before, which was absolutely devastating.

She closed the door behind them, pressing it shut against the building winds. "Feels like that cold front's coming."

Matt set down his gear by the center island in the kitchen. "Precisely why I should get dressed."

She blinked and bit her tongue to keep herself from saying something idiotic. Like, *no, please, stay half naked for me.* The sad truth was, this was the most action she'd had in months. In fact, it was the most action she'd had since Matt.

He cocked his chin sideways and grinned. "I already put my things in the conch room, but we can work all that out later after we talk."

"Good plan."

He excused himself, and Sarah face-palmed, sinking onto a bar stool at the center island. Matt Salvatore. Unbelievable. She never thought she'd see him again. Certainly not as much of him as *that.*

Matt shut the door behind him and slowly shook his head. Sarah Anderson, all after this time. She was the one person he never thought he'd see again. She'd certainly given him the boot sternly enough, and once things got rocky between Elaine and Robert, there wasn't really any occasion to see her. The newlywed couple stopped having folks over shortly after their wedding. Come to think of it, they hadn't entertained much at all. It seemed they were too busy biting each other's heads off to consider serving up dinner to outsiders. It wasn't that Elaine and Robert didn't like each other. In fact, they'd been madly in love. The trouble was both were headstrong individuals, each used to getting his or her own way. This made for some heavy fireworks when even a discussion of which placemats to set on the table sparked an altercation.

Matt extracted his clothes from the dresser, knowing Elaine and Robert's parting had been for the best. The moment they'd split up, they'd seemed like old friends again, not that they wanted to spend much time around each other. Too many unhappy memories of what their tainted married life had been like. Still, neither harbored ill will toward the other, and each was happy to let the other go on with his or her life. The only real thing that bound them together was this beach house at the Outer Banks.

Matt stepped into his jeans, considering the situation. He supposed he should offer to go. That was the gentlemanly thing to do. After all, this was supposed to be Elaine's week here, not Robert's. And what a shame that was too. The fishing today had been mighty fine. Matt even thought he felt that first hint of beard stubble poking through. He'd nearly forgotten how peaceful this place could be, gulls calling and darting above white-capped waves. Matt stared out the window at the tumultuous ocean suddenly shrouded in dark clouds. Seeing Sarah again had turned him inside out in a way he couldn't have expected. He'd nearly forgotten about her completely until he'd looked in those big brown eyes. And, when he had, every inch of him remembered holding her close as they'd swayed to that sultry ballad by a small jazz band. He could even recall the scent of her, fresh and womanly, like daisies after the rain. And those skies had opened up and poured on him all right, sending him packing during the cloudburst. He tugged on his sweatshirt, thinking that this time he'd be more prepared. Sarah wouldn't need to tell him to leave. He was volunteering.

Sarah peered into her cooler, wondering if she should reload it with the cold stuff she'd already stowed in the refrigerator. But her cold packs had melted, so she'd need to stop by the store on the mainland and secure some ice on her way home. It would be rude for her to deplete this place of the one premade bucketful it had. Listen to her! Thinking of being rude to the one man she'd met on the planet who'd proved himself to have no manners. The morning after the wedding, he'd made a quick exit without caring to explain what went wrong. Only one picture bloomed crystal clear in her mind, that of the irresistible best man leaning forward to lift her bridesmaid's dress over her shoulders. How could he when she wasn't even in her right mind? Well, maybe he hadn't been in his either. They'd both *did* have quite a bit of champagne.

The door cracked open to the right-hand master bedroom. There were two large ones in this house, one on either side of the central living area, and each was decorated in its own ocean theme. One sported sand dollars, while the other, the one in which Matt was staying, was adorned in conch shells. He emerged, and Sarah caught her breath on the impossible. He looked just as good fully dressed as he had standing near naked in a towel. She felt her face redden, fearing he could read those thoughts.

As Matt approached, she noticed a backpack casually slung over his shoulder.

There was a small tug at her heart, something akin to pain. Maybe the thought of him walking out conjured up some mysterious sense of déjà vu. But that was silly. Shouldn't she be grateful at his efforts to make things easy?

He set down the backpack and started gathering his fishing gear. "I think it would be simpler if I just went."

"I thought we were going to discuss it?"

He met her gaze with a placating smile. "I'm not sure what's left to discuss. This place was apparently double-booked. Since this wasn't Robert's week to begin with, I'm the one who should go."

Thunder boomed outside and lightning crackled, sending splinters of light throughout the kitchen. Matt packed his cooler. "Sounds like that storm's moving in even sooner than expected."

Sarah peered through the kitchen window at dark clouds rolling over the horizon. In the past few minutes alone, the weather had changed dramatically, though that often happened out here on this little-known barrier island that lay in close proximity to a broad expanse of others. The house sat on a narrow stretch of sand between the ocean and the sound and was accessible only by four-wheel-drive vehicles carried over on a ferry. No roads came out this far, and the rough-hewn trails worn flat by tire tracks were often washed over during heavy rains. A double booking was one thing, but she couldn't have Matt braving the precarious trek back to the boat during a storm. "Maybe it's not safe to drive." As if to accentuate that point, the wind picked up, rattling the screen door.

He strode to the sink beside her and peeked out the window as well. "It's even darker over the sound." Just then the sky opened up, releasing a broad curtain of rain.

"Looks like you came back from fishing just in time," Sarah said.

"Seems like aborting your walk was a good idea."

She stared into mesmerizing blue eyes, and her heart skipped a beat. Did this mean he would stay? At least for a little while?

"I do think I should wait to get on the road. At least until this blows over."

Thunder boomed and rain drove down harder, smacking against the tin roof. "Conditions could be worse later."

"Then again, they could improve."

She didn't know how driving in the dark would make things any better. That wasn't really safe to do around here, even on a clear night. Surely Matt knew that too. "I don't see how," she said, her voice catching in her throat.

He smiled, giving that sexy tilt to his lips.

She reached out a hand to steady herself against the counter.

"Since you're stuck with me awhile, we might as well eat something." He cocked his chin in the direction of her grocery sacks. "Bring any wine in those bags?"

"A few bottles of white." She reached in a bag and produced the evidence. "And, oh yes. A nice big bottle of Chianti."

He grinned, and Sarah's foolish heart went all aflutter. "You pour, and I'll cook dinner."

At the moment, a glass of wine sounded good. If she didn't fear Matt would be counting, she might even have two. But her plus Matt Salvatore—plus alcohol—equaled trouble. She hadn't quite forgotten that. This time, Sarah would have to keep her wits about her and watch every step. For there was really no way around it. Unless there was a dramatic break in the weather soon, the handsome heartbreaker was staying the night.

Chapter Three

Sarah set down her fork and dabbed her pretty mouth with a napkin. "That was absolutely delicious. The best fish I've tasted in ages."

"I just hope I didn't use up too many of our rations in preparing the wine sauce." He lifted the bottle of chardonnay between them, offering to pour her another glass. She declined with a shake of her head.

"I don't think I'd better, thanks."

The deluge continued outdoors, slamming the house with fierce winds that howled in from the ocean and ripped in torrents across the sound. Their small refuge was a battering ram in the eye of the storm but fortunately had been built sturdy enough to withstand it. Over dinner, Matt had learned that Sarah now worked as an interior designer. It was an ambition she'd held since she was a little girl who'd meticulously stylized her dolls' houses. The last time he'd seen her, she'd been considering leaving her stint as a receptionist for a political magazine and finally realizing her dream. She'd found a paid internship at a small design company in Northern Virginia and had eventually worked her way up. Sarah was glad to now have clients all over the District and in parts of Maryland as well, and Matt was proud of her for achieving her goal.

While she was just as beautiful as before, in some ways she seemed more mature, like she'd gained inner confidence. And Matt found that self-assurance intoxicating. He started to pour himself another glass of wine but then thought better of it. With Sarah sitting across from him in the candlelight, her dark eyes catching their glow, he was already feeling light-headed. No sense mixing his emotions up further by stirring in alcohol.

She stood to clear the table, then turned toward the oceanfront window, which was streaked by heavy slogs of rain. "I doubt that they're running the ferry."

"I'll bet that ferry stopped running hours ago," he said, standing and scooping up some plates as well. How he wished he had a clue as to what went wrong all that time ago. Perhaps if he got up the nerve tonight, he'd ask her. He clearly wasn't going anywhere in this weather. Not only was the ferry bound to be cancelled, the beach road that led to the dock was sure to be knee-deep in water right now. Even if the squall magically stopped at this moment, it would take several hours for the storm surge to subside.

Sarah walked to the kitchen and set some dishes in the sink. "It's fine with me if you stay here," she said, color dusting her cheeks.

Matt set his plates on the counter and touched her arm.

She turned toward him.

"I really don't have any other place to go."

She flushed more brilliantly now, slightly catching her breath. "Of course, I know that. I mean, it's silly to think… What I mean is, naturally you should stay. There really are no two ways about it."

"No."

She nervously turned on the water and began scrubbing dishes with a furor, her dish brush circling around and around again in exactly the same spot. Water streamed from the tap, growing hotter, steaming her face, and adding spring to her tight curls.

"Sarah?"

"Huh?" She lifted her brow, appearing surprisingly domestic, standing there by the sink very nearly about to scald herself.

Matt leaned forward and shut off the tap. "I think that one's done."

She stared into the shiny white plate, vaguely spying her reflection. "Uh, yup."

"Tell you what," he said kindly. "Why don't you leave the rest of them for me."

"Really?" she asked, appearing relieved.

He motioned to the plate she'd just finished drying. "After all, you've already done your share."

Sarah was glad to have the opportunity to move to the living area and get out of the kitchen. *If you can't stand the heat, indeed...* Sitting across the table from Matt had proved dangerous enough. What with his easy demeanor and good-natured laughter, it was simple to recall why she'd developed that raging crush on him.

"Can I fix you some tea?"

"Tea would be great," she said, settling on the sofa.

"How about peppermint, in honor of the season?"

"Perfect!" She didn't know what it was about Matt being near that made her such a ball of nerves, but somehow, when he stood close, her heart pounded faster and all reason seemed to evaporate like a wafting soap bubble. Thank goodness he'd sent her out of the kitchen before she'd done some serious damage to herself or the tableware.

Sarah tried to relax and tell herself she was getting all worked up over nothing. So what if she and Matt had a past and he was spending the night? They were two adults and certainly could handle it. It wasn't like there weren't two master bedrooms here.

Sarah nabbed a magazine off the coffee table and casually tried to survey its contents, but her gaze kept traveling away from the copy and homing in on Matt's muscled back. Even through his cable-knit sweater, she could make out its contours, broad shoulders holding steady as he went about his work. He opened a cabinet and stretched tall to grab a teapot off a high shelf, jeans taut across his athletic backside. Sarah recalled that same derriere rising from their cozy bed, clad in nothing but checkered boxers, and felt her temperature rise.

"Doing all right?" he asked, turning toward her as she fanned herself with the magazine.

"Just a little warm in here."

"Warm? I was about to say that it's getting chilly. Suggest we build a fire."

"Great idea," Sarah said, tugging off her too-warm sweater.

Matt set the kettle on the stove, wondering what she was so hellfire nervous about. Okay, so maybe they'd had a bit of a history. But that was years ago. Surely she was over it by now. He was, wasn't he? When they'd tumbled into bed, Matt had thought of nothing more than taking Sarah in his arms. Kissing her soundly. Making love to her... Matt's neck flashed hot at the memory. There'd been something almost hypnotic about her, and the way their bodies had molded together on the dance floor had held the promise of something more. He'd secretly liked her since that first wedding party held on Elaine's outdoor patio. Elaine and Robert had just gotten engaged and wanted to share their newfound joy with a close circle of friends. As it turned out, the dinner guests were also top picks for the wedding party, with Sarah selected as the maid of honor and Matt designated as the best man. He'd taken Sarah a beer, spouting some stupid line about how that meant they'd be working together. She'd narrowed her eyes with a laugh and said, *"Don't bet on us working together too closely."* From that moment, he'd been desperate to hold her and learn more about what made her beautiful brain tick. Sarah wasn't just the best-looking woman in the place, she was also funny and fiery, a bright mischief burning behind those pretty brown eyes. He'd flirted with her all evening and at every prenuptial event after. It wasn't until the wedding reception that she'd finally caved just a little, indicating that all along she'd equally been interested in him.

"You going to get that?"

Matt blinked hard at the kettle squealing on the stovetop before him. He'd been so lost in his reverie, he hadn't heard it go off. "Yeah, sure," he replied as casually as he could. "Just waiting on things to get nice and hot."

Sarah's eyes flashed. "It... I meant, the water... Yeah."

He shot her a tight smile, then turned his back on her to make tea. Hang on, this wasn't right. All this while he'd been thinking she was the skittish one, but just look at him. *Let's build a fire… Let things get nice and hot.* If he was going to come on to her, he could at least man up and do it directly. Not that this was in his plan. It hadn't been his idea to walk out last time. Sarah had been the one to tell him to hit the road. And, given that the roads around here were certainly washed over, Matt decided that now wasn't the time to bring up any touchy-feely subjects.

He strode across the living room with two steaming mugs of tea and sat down beside her, handing one over. Nearly imperceptibly, she rearranged herself on the sofa, scooting just the tiniest bit away from him. This was it, then. No sign could be clearer than that. Sarah wasn't any more interested in Matt getting close than she'd been three years ago. Fine. He could deal with that. He was just here for one night, anyway.

Sarah took a sip of peppermint tea as the rain beat down harder and the winds wailed. "It's delicious. Thank you."

"I'm sorry?" he said beneath the commotion slamming their cottage from every direction.

Sarah raised her voice just a tad. "I said thanks for the tea! It's delicious."

"Glad that you like it," Matt called back. The lights flickered, and they both stared at each other.

"You don't think we'll lose power, do you?"

"Robert put in a generator," Matt said in an effort to reassure her. But all Sarah could think of was being alone here. With Matt. In the dark. It was hard enough to resist him with all the lights blazing, Sarah thought, feeling overheated again. She inched away from him on the sofa, then laughed when he gave her a quizzical look.

"Just getting comfortable, that's all." As if to prove it, she stuffed a large throw pillow behind her back. "Ah. Much better!"

Matt drank from his tea, then set it down. "Hmm. Yes."

"When do you think they'll reopen the ferry?"

"I suppose as soon as the water calms down."

Outside the large glass door, the ocean tumbled about furiously, giving no indication that would be anytime soon. "Sarah," Matt said, studying her sincerely. "I don't want you to worry. Don't think anything will happen here just because you and I—"

"No, of course not," she rushed in, feeling idiotic.

"I mean, we do have separate bedrooms, after all."

"I know," she answered, wishing with all her might he hadn't said that. Bedrooms plus Matt Salvatore in her mind led to one terribly embarrassing memory. Not that she totally blamed her formerly drunken self. She'd been a little younger and a whole less wiser back then. These days she understood what keeping her distance meant. It meant steering clear of unnecessary temptation. She picked up her tea, standing. "I think I'd better carry this back to the bedroom. Start unpacking."

Matt's brow creased with concern. "Did I say something...?"

"Oh no, it's nothing like that. It's just been a long day."

She stared into deep blue eyes, consumed by them. He was one good-looking man, maybe the best-looking one she'd ever seen. It was impossible not to remember what it was like to kiss him and how his mouth had moved over hers with obviously practiced skill.

He held her gaze, and her heart stilled. "I hear you," he said below the tumult of the storm. "Sleep well."

When she spoke, she found her voice a little breathless. "Will this place be in one piece tomorrow?" But the truth was, she was more worried about her heart than the house getting lost in the squall.

"I'm sure we'll be fine. This house has withstood far worse and lived to tell the tale."

It was impossible for Sarah to sleep with the winds wailing outdoors. Each time the house shook, she feared for their security, imagining their tiny cottage being swept out to sea in a swell. But that was ludicrous. Matt was right. This place had been built to withstand the winds. And this wasn't some huge hurricane anyway. It was nothing more than a fierce winter storm tearing its way down the east coast. Winds howled again, sending the window casings rattling in her room, and Sarah sat up with a start. An eerie light illuminated the room, emanating from the solar-powered nightlight placed in a low wall outlet. No way could she settle down now. Maybe some more of that herb tea would help.

Sarah slid out from under the covers and tugged a sweatshirt over her head. It had grown chilly in the midst of the storm, a damp cold seeping indoors. She'd be warmer sleeping with someone else but wasn't about to consider it. Falling into bed at the drop of a hat wasn't her style. This was one reason her escapade with Matt had proved so jarring. While she wasn't precisely chaste, she'd slept only with the few guys with whom she'd had committed relationships. Bedding the best man had been an outlier. So far outside her realm of normal behavior, in fact, that it had caused her to question her priorities. And when she examined those, she saw that what she longed for most of all wasn't some guy who was in it for a one-night stand. She wanted a guy who would stick around forever, in sickness and in health. Someone who wouldn't turn tail and run the moment he learned more about her.

Sarah sighed, wishing so much that Matt had proved himself to be different. But he'd been like all the rest. Eager to take advantage and then ride off into the sunrise at the first crack of dawn. Of course, she understood she was equally to blame for their night of debauchery. It was just a pity that—after all the trouble it had caused—she couldn't recall the details.

Matt rummaged through the cabinets in search of something to eat. He didn't know why he was so incredibly hungry, but his stomach had been growling so loudly he hadn't been able to sleep. Perhaps he hadn't had enough dinner, or maybe it was nerves. Growing up in a big Italian family had taught him that the best way to settle any insecurity was with a hearty dose of food. But why should Matt feel unsettled at all? It wasn't like he had to worry about becoming involved with Sarah. She clearly had no greater interest in him now than she'd had previously. And that was a shame too. The truth was she'd never given him a chance. *Never given us a chance...to see what might be.* He couldn't imagine what he'd done wrong, but she hadn't even wanted to talk about it. At least she'd been upfront in saying good-bye. Conniving Katya would have kept him coming back for more, as long as he'd failed to discover her duplicity.

He set a box of crackers on the counter and opened the refrigerator in search of some cheese, believing he'd think better after a snack. He didn't know what it was about Sarah that still got to him after all this time. For all intents and purposes, she was a small part of his past. A long-lost flirtation he should have written off over the years. But seeing her again had proved something different. Matt had an odd inner instinct that maybe there was a reason... Some convoluted explanation for why they'd wound up here together. He wondered vaguely if she was sensing this too. Or whether he'd only imagined Sarah's warm brown eyes registering interest as she'd held his gaze, saying good night.

Sarah padded toward the kitchen in her slippers thinking she'd heard noises there. But it was after two in the morning. Surely Matt couldn't be up? She rounded the corner, then stopped in her tracks. It was Matt standing nude on the far side of the open refrigerator door! All she could spy from her position was the top of his gloriously muscled chest, bare shoulders, and his deep blue eyes peering in her direction.

"Sarah?" he asked with surprise. "What are you doing up?"

She took a giant step back, hands to her cheeks, which felt as hot as coals. "I…uh…" She dropped her hands with a questioning look. "What are *you* doing up?"

He glanced downward as if checking something, then once again met her eyes. It was pretty hard to tell in the dim light of the kitchen, but Sarah could almost swear his face had colored as well. "I'm just getting a snack."

"Do you always eat naked?" she blurted out, the words racing off her tongue.

A slow, sly grin worked its way across his sexy face. "Not usually," he said, shutting the refrigerator door.

Sarah gasped and shut her eyes. "Ah!"

She'd hoped she would hear him making his retreat. Or at least, goodness knows, grabbing a dishtowel. Instead she just heard silence, coupled with competing winds.

"Well, they may be a little ratty, but I don't think my camp shorts look that bad."

Sarah peeked between splayed fingers to see he was right. In fact, what he wore—something akin to boxers—made him look absolutely terrific. He smiled and held out some cheese. "I was just sitting down for a bite. Want to join me?"

"Will there be wine involved?" she asked, thinking she needed it badly. Not a whole lot, just a small glass. Enough to calm her nerves—and erase the picture she'd just envisioned.

"There could be."

"Do you think you could put a few more clothes on?"

He laughed warmly. "Anything you'd like. Do you prefer jeans or sweatpants?"

"Doesn't matter," she said, feeling her cheeks warm again.

"Why don't you pick the wine while I go change?"

Sarah found the corkscrew with unsteady fingers. Staying here alone with Matt wasn't nearly as easy as she'd imagined. Every time he centered those gorgeous blue eyes on hers, the memories came racing back. Most of them, anyhow.

"Still don't have it open yet?" Matt asked, resurfacing in record time. He wore jeans and an old gray sweatshirt. Only his feet were bare as before.

Sarah grimaced, wrestling with the bottle. "Cork seems to be stuck."

"Here, let me help with that."

He stepped forward to take the bottle, and Sarah's heart beat faster. It was hard to forget what being in his arms had been like. More impossible still to erase the memory of his kiss.

Matt easily opened the wine and poured them each a glass. Once he'd set some cheese and crackers on a platter, they each settled down on one of the barstools abutting the center island.

"I'm sorry I walked in on you that way," Sarah began.

"Don't be. It wasn't your fault. You had no way to know I was out here."

"No."

It niggled at Sarah that neither of them had brought up their previous night together. Her practical side longed to finally clear the air, but her more emotional self wasn't sure she could take it. Being told by a guy why you weren't appealing to him was never a joy. Although she'd guessed her besotted behavior had something to do with it, she'd always had a feeling there'd been something more. Something else about that evening she hadn't completely understood.

They sat for a moment in awkward silence, both nibbling on cheese and crackers as the storm continued to rage outdoors. At this pace, there'd be no getting out of here tomorrow, or maybe even the day after that. Though it was hard to focus on leaving with the soft light from the kitchen surrounding Sarah in its homey glow. She looked so sweet sitting there in her pajama pants and sweatshirt, just like a vision from a dream. He'd watched her dreaming once before.

"Sarah?" he asked, then sipped from his wine. "Can I ask you a question?"

"I don't see why not."

"Why did you tell me to go?"

She glanced at him, taken aback, as if she hadn't expected the question. "Me?"

"Yes. You. And that was after a whole night of you begging me to—"

"Matt, I don't see why you..." She set down her wine, seeming to grow uncomfortable. "What I mean is, that's all ancient history."

He set down his wine as well and laid his hand on top of hers. "Is it?"

Her cheeks colored slightly. "I'm not sure what you want me to say. That wasn't me. I'm normally not like that."

"Let's hope not!" he said with a laugh.

She withdrew her hand, affronted. "What do you mean?"

"All sick and pukey? Most girls wouldn't want to live through that twice."

"Sick and...?" Her voice fell off with the shock.

"Yes, Sarah. You were deathly ill. All over your bridesmaid's dress, in fact. I had to take it off to clean it."

"I what?"

"That's probably why you repeatedly begged me to *please forget this in the morning.*"

"I said that?"

"Well, yeah, between, you know..." He motioned with his hands, and she got the picture. "Not that I totally blamed you. I wasn't up for remembering certain parts of it myself. Hang on, are you saying you don't remember?"

She shook her head, her cheeks blazing brightly.

"Not even the part about making me swear I'd leave, just get out of your life, and never breathe a word about it to anybody?"

She pursed her lips, struggling with a murky memory. "I remember making you swear, swear…something." Big brown eyes met his. "But to be honest with you, Matt, most of the night is a great big blur."

"Then it's a good thing nothing happened between us," he said, lightly teasing. "For most men, that admission could be a killer."

Her eyes lit with understanding. "So…we didn't?"

"No." He cocked his chin to the side. "We didn't. Not that I didn't want to, mind you. Especially when we first got back to your place, and you kissed me like a house on fire. Heck, I'm only human. But, I wouldn't have. Never like that. Not once I realize your condition."

"And all this time I thought…" She heaved a sigh of relief. "But, no?"

"Is that why you told me to leave?" he asked, his voice growing husky with the truth. "Because you thought I'd taken advantage of you?"

"I never blamed you. I thought it was both of us."

"Oh, it was both of us, all right. Just not in the way that you imagined."

She stared at him deeply, apology in her eyes. "I'm so sorry. I had no idea."

"I had no idea either," he said softly. "No clue why you gave me the boot. While you'd told me to go throughout the night, I'd taken that to be the liquor—and possibly embarrassment—talking. I thought for sure once you woke up and saw things straight, we'd talk things out, maybe even laugh about them. But instead, you just handed me my coat and said—"

"I think you should go." She hung her head, seeming to relive the moment.

"The truth is, I thought that we'd been getting along. Maybe had started something."

She raised her eyes to his. In the ensuing quiet, Matt thought he could hear every drop of rain pinging on the tin roof. When she finally spoke, her lips trembled, and it was all Matt could do not to lean forward and kiss them. "I thought we'd started something too. But sometimes life has other plans, you know?"

He nodded like he understood, but the truth of the matter was he didn't. "Was there somebody else at the time?"

She shook her head. "How about you?"

"Not then, for me either." He studied her for a long beat. "And now?"

"I'm not seeing anyone, if that's what you mean."

He captured her in his gaze, wondering if there was a way they could start over. There had clearly been an attraction between them in the beginning. "Me either."

"Matt," she said sincerely, "I really apologize for what happened that night, and also for the way I judged you afterward. It wasn't fair. None of it was fair. I see that now."

"We all make mistakes."

One of the biggest he'd made was failing to pursue things with Sarah. He might have called the next day. Attempted to see her. Instead, he'd just up and walked away from what could have been the best thing in his life. Then, within the next few weeks, he'd met Katya.

"Thank you for saying that. That's really gracious, considering the trouble I put you through."

"No trouble. I'm sure you would have done the same," he said, knowing that would have proved logistically difficult. Matt tried to imagine the petite Sarah hoisting his large frame across the room and depositing it in bed, and chuckled out loud.

"I know," she said, smiling softly. "Pretty hard to imagine, huh?"

"Yeah."

"How do you think the roads will look tomorrow?"

"I'll check at first light."

Chapter Four

The next morning, Matt bent toward the washed-out road, wearing his rain slicker. Water streamed from the front of his hood, cascading down his nose. It was still pouring. Somehow it seemed twice as hard as yesterday. Nobody could get traction on this stretch of beach now. Not even a ranger's four-wheel drive could do it. He was here for the duration. Another day or two at least. He supposed he'd have to break the news to Sarah but hoped she wouldn't take it badly. She'd seemed more at ease in his company this morning, after they'd cleared the air about Elaine's wedding last night. Perhaps her appearing on edge before had to do with her misunderstanding what had really happened. Matt felt a whole lot better fully knowing what had happened as well.

He glanced back toward the house through a curtain of rain as thunder rumbled above. Bright light burned through each window, like warming lanterns speckling the storm. If things looked this bad here, they could be even worse down at the docks. He'd need to call and check on the status of the ferry. He figured Sarah would want to make it home for Christmas Day with her family, and he'd more or less promised Robert he'd share it with him and his wife. For the moment, though, he'd just need to make his way indoors to keep from getting further drenched.

"How does it look?" she asked when Matt stepped inside.

Matt removed his dripping coat and held it outside the door, shaking it hard. "Not good. That road won't be passable today."

"Oh." Sarah tried to frame her response as mild disappointment, but inwardly her mood lightened. All night long, she'd relived Matt's words telling her he wasn't taken, as if he'd been hinting he wanted to give things with her another go. It was possible she'd misread his signals. There was an equal chance that, even if she hadn't, she wasn't fully ready. Ready to take the risk of telling the truth to yet another man.

Matt picked up the landline mounted on the kitchen wall and started to dial. "I think I'd better call the ferry and see what the status of things is there."

While Sarah couldn't hear the other side of the conversation, she could imagine as Matt creased his brow and said, "Uh-huh. Um-hmm. I see.

"I'm sorry, Sarah," he told her, hanging up the phone. "It seems the docks took quite a beating. They don't think the boat will be running again before the end of the week."

"End of the week? But that means—"

"Looks like we're stuck here for Christmas." He shrugged apologetically. "I'm sure that's the last thing you had in mind."

Actually, the only plans that she had involved spending another uncomfortable holiday with her mom and her mom's new boyfriend. Not that they *tried* to make her feel in the way. It was just that it was pretty clear they enjoyed spending time alone, making Sarah feel like a third wheel. A lovely fantasy began unfolding before her... Just her and Matt, and a big, wonderful Christmas tree, dotted with shiny lights... Then reality sank in, and Sarah realized they had no tree or presents or stockings to hang from the mantel. And here she was acting like she'd already had three hits of eggnog. With bourbon! "Are you sure?" she asked, trying not to sound overly hopeful.

Matt studied her with a frown. "You're pretty disappointed. I can understand that. You probably have family plans."

Her mom didn't even decorate for Christmas and had never really believed in the holiday for myriad reasons. So, they typically ordered take-out Chinese and watched a movie in front of the fake fire. That was the only sort of family holiday Sarah was used to.

"My family's plans will likely go on without me," she answered truthfully. "But what about yours?"

Matt laughed, stepping out of his drenched boots. "Oh, I think Robert, Margaret, and their new baby will manage just fine."

"You weren't planning to go to Chicago?" she asked, remembering the large, happy family she'd met at Elaine's first wedding.

"My brother and sisters and I sent our folks on an anniversary trip to Tuscany this year. It's their fortieth anniversary."

"Oh, how sweet!" she said, meaning it absolutely. Sarah tried but couldn't imagine what that would be like. Being a part of such a warm, loving family and having parents who'd stayed together for that many years. She didn't even remember her father, and her mom refused to say much about him. The men she remembered growing up with were a series of short-term boyfriends for her mom, none of whom ever stuck around. Sarah had liked one of the early ones when she'd been a kid. His name had been Joey, and he'd a few daughters of his own. He was a kind man who'd seemed to take an interest in Sarah from the start. He took her out for ice cream with his own girls and had even taught her how to ride a bike. He'd been a good guy but somehow not good enough for her mom. She'd thrown him over for Fred just about the time Sarah got off her training wheels.

"Don't you think Robert and Margaret will miss you?"

"With that new little bundle to keep them busy?" he said with a smile. "Not a chance."

Lightning crackled, and Sarah stared out the rain-streaked window. "So, what do we do?"

Matt carted his backpack toward his bedroom with a wink. "Make the best of it."

After a soup and sandwich lunch, Sarah found herself chatting easily with Matt before a roaring fire. She'd made them coffee while he'd gotten the fire started, and now they sat discussing their afternoon plans. They'd already had a great time sorting through the house's stash of holiday movies and board games, so they had a sense of what type of entertainment was in store. Being stuck here with Matt wasn't going to prove uncomfortable at all. In fact, Sarah decided it could be a whole lot of fun. Just as long as she could keep her heart in check, she thought with a sigh.

"So, what's on the agenda?"

"Well, I don't think we'll be swimming today," he said with a teasing smile.

"No. You're probably right about that. I think it's cold enough to snow out there."

"Now that would be something, wouldn't it?"

"Snow at the beach? It happens."

"Yeah, it happens. But around here, it's rare."

She smiled above the rim of her cup, enjoying their light banter. They'd both phoned their families to explain neither would be coming home, and incredibly, everyone seemed happy with the situation. As long as they were safe and had enough provisions to weather the storm, everybody understood. In fact, they were glad that Matt and Sarah had serendipitously wound up there together. How much nicer for the two of them that each wouldn't have to spend Christmas alone. "So maybe we'll have a white Christmas?"

"Ha! You'll have to ask Santa for that." He mischievously cocked one eyebrow and studied her. "Don't tell me you're too old to believe in Santa?"

Sarah thumbed her chest. "Me? No. It's just that I've never had the pleasure."

"Of what?"

"Meeting Santa. Knowing him, whatever."

He stared at her aghast. "Are you telling me, not even as a kid?"

Sarah shook her head. "Cheryl doesn't believe in such."

"Cheryl?"

"My mom. She wanted me to start calling her Cheryl when I was, oh…about eleven."

"Really? Why?"

"Once I hit puberty…" She felt her face flush. "Well, I guess the thought of having a daughter my age made her feel old."

"Ouch."

"It's okay. I got over it."

"Not having a mom?"

"Oh, I had a mom. She was just…different. You know?"

He nodded like he was trying to understand, but Sarah didn't see how he could completely. Not coming from the background he did, which was so diametrically different. "So, what about Christmas, then? If there was no Santa, how did you celebrate?"

"Generally with moo shu pork and gas logs."

"Were you happy that way?"

"It was the only way I knew. I mean, sure. I heard the other kids in school bragging about what they got for Christmas and stuff, but after a while I learned not to worry about it. My mom always got me what I needed and didn't want to fill my head with bubble-headed fantasies anyway."

"Like the notion of Santa Claus and make-believe and dreaming impossible dreams?"

"Yes."

Matt's gaze was lined with compassion. He was trying to read her, and Sarah felt as open as a book. "I see."

"It wasn't so bad, really," she said, trying to lighten the moment.

Matt smiled at her, his face brightening. "No, I'm sure it wasn't. Who's to say which way is better? One person's childhood or another? I had a big brother to beat up on me."

"Robert?"

"Yeah, but he did so in a loving way." He shot her a wry smile. "And I still have the scars to prove it."

"Oh!" Sarah replied, not knowing whether he was kidding.

"So, come on," he said. "Let's decide what's next. Between the two of us, we've clearly brought enough provisions to get by. But did either of us plan for anything fun?"

"Fun?"

"Yeah, you know. Something to get us in the holiday spirit?"

"Well," Sarah began tentatively, "I had planned to make Christmas cookies while I was here. Take them home for the holiday."

"Perfect!" Matt said with a grin. "I'm in."

A little while later, Sarah found herself standing at the kitchen counter with Matt. He'd located Robert's CD collection and put on some music. With it turned up loud, they could scarcely hear the howling winds below the sultry collection labeled *Rainy Day Blues.* Nothing could have been more appropriate. Waves crashed outdoors and windy gusts slammed the house, though inside they were safe and warm.

"Well, go on," he said. "Lay it on me."

She looked up at him, and her knees went weak. All this light chatter with Matt had gone right to her head just like a million champagne bubbles. He was so easy to be with. Fun and lighthearted too. Was it any wonder she'd crushed on him so badly three years ago? But now she was getting to know him better—which made things worse. If only she could believe that certain things wouldn't matter to him.

"The supplies?" he said, reading her dumbstruck look. "What did you bring?"

"Oh, that," she said, feeling she sounded a bit dopey. This was crazy, and she knew it. All they were doing here was making Christmas cookies. It wasn't like they were slathering each other all over with icing. Her face flamed hot as she feared he'd read her thoughts. Of course she wouldn't be coating Matt with icing. *That* was to be reserved for the cookies. But wasn't he a dish? *Yummy.*

"Sarah?"

She swallowed hard, collecting herself. Before they'd started to cook, Matt had offered to serve some wine. After all, they still had that open bottle from their late-night snacking... At the time, she'd been feeling so good and confident in her abilities to resist him that this had sounded fine. Now Sarah wondered if that had been such a great idea.

"Ah, yeah," she said, opening the refrigerator to retrieve the limp tube of sugar-cookie dough. She absolutely, positively, had to get herself under control.

Matt looked down at the dough, then right in her eyes. "Slice and bake?"

"I brought icing," she said lamely, hoping he couldn't read between the lines.

Matt took the cookie dough from her and set it on the counter, shutting the refrigerator door. "Do you mean to tell me you've never made sugar cookies from scratch?"

"Well, no," she said feeling her face warm with embarrassment. "No, actually I haven't. Is that a problem?"

He slowly stroked his chin and studied her. "No, darling, it's not a problem at all. I was just wondering..." His lips creased in a subtle smile. "If you'd like to learn?"

"What do you mean?" she asked, taken aback.

"I have confession to make," he said. His voice was low and raspy. "I'm one helluva baker."

She sputtered a laugh. "Go on!"

"I'm also a dynamite teacher."

Was it sheer coincidence that in the background a song about giving love lessons started to play? Matt could teach her all right, probably a lot of things. A man like him was sure to have had his share of the ladies.

"Are you now?" she said, backing up a step.

He'd be damned if she didn't look enticing, just standing there with that little pout on her lips. Matt took another sip of wine, tuned in to the music. "You're not afraid?"

"Of learning something new?" She pulled herself up a little straighter and squared her shoulders. "Of course not."

That was all the encouragement he needed to grab an apron off a nearby hook and tie it on. "Did you bring any sugar?"

"I brought a small container, enough for what I use in my coffee."

She produced the square Tupperware, and he whistled. "Got quite a sweet tooth, have you?"

Her cute face reddened all over. "I brought extra."

"Well, that's good, extra good. And, I'm betting we both brought butter." He grinned, his enthusiasm building. He was going to do this. Teach Sarah to bake cookies from scratch. Even if forcing himself to keep his hands off her sumptuous body killed him. Man, didn't she look sexy offering up her sugar that way? "I brought eggs and a bag of flour for coating fried fish."

She gasped as he set it on the counter. "A whole five-pound bag? Got quite an appetite, do you?"

He shook a finger at her and grinned. "Got me there. Now, all we need is vanilla."

"Think there's any in the house?"

He turned to check supplies in the pantry, figuring he could replace anything they used later. After a few seconds passed, he held up a small dark bottle.

"Bingo."

Sarah didn't know how Matt made it all look so easy. They didn't even have cookie cutters, but he'd fashioned some makeshift from various-sized drinking glasses turned upside-down to use their rims as cutting surfaces. "It's incredible how you figured all that out," she told him, duly impressed.

"And you thought I'd only studied law at Georgetown."

"You didn't learn this in law school," she said astutely. "You learned this at home."

"Guilty," he said, not looking culpable in the least. "It was all about food at the Salvatore house, especially with my folks running the restaurant."

"That must have been something," she said a bit wistfully. "Growing up with a big happy family and so many siblings."

"We managed," he said with a grin. "Managed to get into a lot of trouble and drive our parents crazy. Though I understand I'll have this coming back at me one day."

"What do you mean?"

"What goes around comes around. I have no illusions about my own kids not giving me grief, in one way or another, when the time comes. I'll more or less accept it as my due."

It was easy to guess that Matt would make a terrific dad. His life experience had primed him for it. Naturally, he wanted kids. Not five children perhaps, but at least one or two.

"Your turn," he said, handing over the rolling pin. "Why don't you try?"

Sarah took the weighty implement in her hand, not knowing quite what to do with it. Naturally she understood she was to press it to that little ball of dough and flatten it out, but she wasn't so certain her results would come out as stellar at Matt's. The truth was, Sarah had never been instructed much in the way of cooking at all. And, for one reason or another had never felt much inclined to learn. Her mom was a restaurant kind of girl who considered prepackaged dinners sold in the frozen section as good as homemade. She'd probably passed that gene on to Sarah. Nearly everything Sarah ate came out of some sort of box. Not that she was prepared to tell Mr. I'm-Italian-and-Cook-Everything-from-Scratch at the moment. He probably thought she'd only packed frozen foods for her trip to the beach.

"Go on," he said kindly. "Just put your weight into it evenly and give it a go."

Sarah smiled uncertainly over her shoulder. "All right," she said, determined to try. She centered her gaze on the big mound of glop on the counter, wondering how she was going to press that into a perfect one-quarter-inch slab the way he had. She grabbed each handle on the rolling pin and gingerly pressed forward. The blob squished slightly, but the rolling pin stuck. Not much else happened.

"Put your back into it," Matt prodded.

She glanced at him cheering her on from the sidelines and then gave it her all, heaving her might into that little wooden spindle in her hands. Dough splatted out like an egg cracked fresh from its shell, transparently thin on the cutting surface. "Oh no!" she cried with dismay. Even *she* knew there was no way to bake cookies from *that*.

"Here, let me help." He sidled up behind her and calmly collected the mess, transforming it into a new ball. "It's all in the technique," he said, his voice a light tickle at the side of her neck. He drew nearer still, enveloping her in his warmth, and every inch of her came alive. He smelled so good and manly standing so close, the sleeves of his sweatshirt just brushing hers as he positioned himself around her.

He stepped a fraction of an inch closer, and Sarah feared she might faint from his proximity. It was intoxicating being enveloped in his arms, his solid chest pressing into her back as he steadied his hands around hers on the rolling pin. The "Love Lessons" song had ended, and a more provocative one had started to play. "Just like this," he said, swaying forward. She moved with him, letting him lead as dough glided into a flat plane. "And like this…" he whispered in her ear, lifting the rolling pin and repeating the process again as the sexy music played on.

Sarah felt breathless, as if she might faint at any moment, lost in the rhythm of Matt's embrace.

He held her more tightly in his arms and whispered, his voice husky. "What do you think of home cooking?"

In many ways, this felt more intimate than dancing, almost as if they were in bed. But Sarah had never been with a man who moved with such grace and care for her comfort.

"I think I like it," she said, barely breathing the words.

He stopped rolling, wrapping his fingers around hers.

"These are going to be damn good cookies."

"Yes," she agreed.

The seconds ticked by like hours as Sarah's heart beat furiously. Was it her imagination, or could she feel Matt's heart beating in his chest behind her as well? All she could think of was Matt turning her in his arms and kissing her, just as wonderfully as he had on that dance floor all that time ago. But then the kitchen timer went off, indicating the previous batch of cookies had baked.

Matt nestled his chin on her shoulder. "I think we're done."

"What?" she asked, her knees on the verge of collapse. The timer beeped louder, intruding once more on their moment. He lightly squeezed her hands in his.

"The dough, Sarah. It looks like it's perfect."

And it did, a perfect quarter-inch slab. They were ready to cut.

Matt broke his embrace and headed for the oven, which couldn't have burned any hotter than she felt right now.

Sarah excused herself for a moment and strode quickly to her bathroom, where she splashed cold water on her face. Then, she dampened a washcloth to dab the front, sides, and back of her neck. That Matt Salvatore was one hot man in the kitchen. Look at the mess she was in, and all from one teeny little glass of wine. But inwardly Sarah knew it hadn't just been the alcohol that had sent her head spinning and her heart racing. That had more to do with being deliciously wrapped up in the sexy Italian's arms while moving to that sultry music. When he captured her in his deep blue gaze, liquor was beside the point. She was drunk on him,

Matt Salvatore the man, and all the wonderful things he was.

And one of those, Sarah reminded herself sternly, was someone who wanted to be a father. She swallowed hard, gathering her nerve to go back out there and face him. She needed to nix the wine and find a way to get through the rest of this day on more even footing. Perhaps she could offer to fix dinner and shoo Matt out of the kitchen for the next little while. There was clearly too much combustible heat in the room for the two of them. Then after dinner, maybe they could do something harmless like watch a holiday movie. One of those funny family films. Romance, right now, was a no-go. It was simple to see how quickly she could fall for Matt. The scary thing was, Sarah worried that she'd started falling already. She needed to stop herself before she got in deeper, in order to avoid a most certain and devastating outcome. Walking away from Matt with a broken heart.

The second Sarah had cleared the room, Matt set the cookie tray on the stovetop and pulled an ice cube from the freezer, pressing it to the back of his flaming neck. It melted on contact, sending little dribbles racing down the line of his back. Sarah had set him virtually on fire. She'd been so subtle and giving in his arms, yielding to his every move. No wonder he'd wanted to take her to bed before. It wasn't just the way she kissed, it was in the sexy way she carried herself, seemed to have complete control of her body. Well…except for that sickness thing. She was definitely out of control then. But everyone's allowed a slipup now and again. He'd had his fair share of his own, particularly in his younger days.

Matt rocked the open freezer door back and forth, rapidly fanning his face with puffs of icy air. It was working already. He was feeling better. Next best thing to a cold shower, he supposed, hoping Sarah hadn't noticed his level of excitement before she'd raced out of here. Or maybe she had, and that was why she'd bolted like a scared rabbit. Matt felt suddenly consumed by guilt, wondering if he'd done something wrong by laying it on so thick. It wasn't exactly like he'd planned their cooking lesson to turn extra hot. It just serendipitously had. Of course, once it had headed in that direction, he'd done nothing overt to stop it. He surely would have if Sarah had protested. Yet she seemed to be enjoying their joint venture into the culinary arts just as much as he had. Matt hoped he hadn't imagined that. He would feel awful if she felt he'd come on too strong and that had put her off. For Matt was growing attracted to Sarah, way attracted. And in his heart of hearts, he couldn't believe he'd gotten her signals that wrong. She was growing attracted to him as well. But Matt needed to be careful not to push it. Maybe the best thing to do would be force himself to back off a bit and let Sarah take the lead. If she was truly as interested as his instinct said, within the next couple of days she definitely would.

Sarah returned looking all fresh-faced with her hair pulled up in a ponytail. By this time, Matt had already washed the baking dishes and was busy putting them away. "I was going to help you with that," she protested, a little after the fact.

"It's all right. I didn't mind it. Besides, the kitchen needed to be tidied before I start dinner."

"Oh no, you don't." Sarah bossily entered the kitchen and took him by the elbow. He set down his dishtowel with surprise. "You've done all the cooking you're going to for the next little while."

He was mildly disappointed by that. Mostly, he'd been hoping they'd do some more cooking together. The good thing was that Sarah appeared bright and cheery, not like she was upset about anything. Perhaps she had enjoyed being close to him but was just too conservative to say so. She handed him his glass of wine and steered him toward the sofa. "Why don't you sit, and I'll refill that for you? I'm doing the cooking tonight."

That sounded super to Matt. He could relax in front of the fire and briefly check the score on the game. "Mind if I turn on some football? Just for a moment."

"Watch it as long as you'd like," she called from the kitchen with a smile. She pulled two frozen pizzas from the freezer, and Matt chuckled to himself, wondering if back in Maryland she did any home cooking at all. Not that it mattered to him. He was sure the dinner would taste just as delicious as if she'd made the pizza dough herself. All he had to do was look in Sarah's eyes and everything seemed better. Even being trapped at the beach in a storm was starting to seem pretty awesome.

Chapter Five

The next day was just as enjoyable. It was still too nasty to go outdoors, with very high winds and lightning. But inside, they found plenty to do. They'd watched a movie together, read companionably by the fire, and had taken turns cooking. Now they were settled at the dining room table, sharing milk and cookies over Holiday Scrabble.

"Not fair!" he challenged with a laugh as she chalked up another triple word score. "You never told me that you were a Scrabble shark."

"It's how you play the game." She playfully met his eyes. "No mercy." She didn't show any either, beating him in a close match. Afterward, they were both tired and ready to call it a day. It had been such a good one, Sarah found herself really looking forward to another with Matt. And what was special about tomorrow was it was Christmas Eve.

"Thanks for another fun day," she said after they'd put away the game.

"Thanks for scorching me in Scrabble. Something tells me I could learn a thing or two from you."

She laughed, feeling lighthearted. The fact was that Matt made her happier than anyone ever had. It was a fantastic feeling, almost like having a partner and friend who was also very easy on the eyes. Sarah cautioned herself against thinking of partnerships with Matt. Once he knew the truth about her, he wouldn't be able to think of her in that way, just as her last serious boyfriend hadn't. "Oh yeah?"

"Yeah." They stood in close proximity now, only inches apart. He stepped forward, closing the small space between them. It was silly to think he might kiss her, but she secretly wished for it just the same. He'd been so gentlemanly in keeping his distance since their cooking lesson, Sarah had started wondering what she'd been doing wrong. Then she reminded herself that things were playing out just the way she'd wanted them to. But if this was the case, why did the outcome leave her feeling sad and conflicted? If only there was a way to make things work, she would find it. But at the moment, everything seemed impossible.

"Sleep tight. I hope you have pleasant dreams."

She held his gaze, knowing her dreams would include him. "You too."

"The storm's supposed to let up tomorrow," he said, his voice raspy.

Sarah's heart skipped a beat. She certainly hoped not. Not if it meant that Matt would be leaving. She was still wrestling with so much in her heart and head, trying to sort everything out. And that was so hard to do with him standing close enough to hold her.

"Of course, even if the roads clear," he continued, "that ferry won't be up and running until late in the week."

Sarah breathed a sigh of relief, remembering. "That's right, the ferry," she said, backing up a step. "Can't go anywhere without the big boat." Wow, didn't he look gorgeous just standing there in all of his studly beauty, a few days of beard stubble lightly framing his face? Never had a man appealed to her so much.

He raised his brow, watching her with amusement.

"You might want to turn around. You might bump into something."

She held up her hand in agreement and whirled on her heels. Quickly enough, she hoped, to disguise her rabid blush. She'd been so intent on ogling Matt she hadn't wanted to take her eyes off of him. Him and that beautiful body and his gorgeous blue eyes. It must have been a subconscious desire, because she hadn't even realized she was doing it.

Sarah ducked behind her bedroom door, closing it with a gasp. Christmas Day was fast approaching, and she could think of only one thing she wanted. Having Matt take her once again in his arms.

Matt approached Sarah as she stood sipping her coffee by the oceanside sliding glass door. She looked beautiful this morning in a pretty pink sweater and slightly worn jeans, her long, loose hair damp from her morning shower.

"Looks like it's still coming down out there," he said, referencing the rain.

"Yeah, but not as hard as before." She smiled sweetly over the rim of her cup, and Matt had the crazy notion that hers was a smile he wouldn't mind seeing at eight in the morning any old time of the year. He was just glad he was getting this unexpected chance to spend the holiday with her. It was way better than intruding on Robert and Margaret's first Christmas as parents. The view was a lot nicer too. And Matt wasn't thinking about the drenched stretch of sand ahead of them.

"Thanks for making the coffee," she said. "It was a treat finding it ready when I got up."

"It's no problem, really. I set it to brew before getting dressed and right after phoning the ferry."

Her delicate brow rose as she turned toward him. "What's the word?" She didn't say it, but Matt could tell she wasn't any more interested in that boat taking off today than he was.

"Still down for the duration." Even though the winds had abated, storm damage to the docks would take some time to repair. Some of it wouldn't even get started until the rain had fully stopped.

"That's too bad," she said, faking her disappointment badly.

"Hmm, yes. A total shame."

He studied her a long while, lost in the heat of her stare. While it didn't seem possible, each time he looked in those dark brown eyes, they appeared even more enticing.

Her pretty mouth drew up at the corners. "You know, I was thinking… I'm feeling a little cage crazy in here."

"Seriously? I was just thinking the same thing." In fact, he'd awakened this morning feeling a dire need to stretch his legs. Get out on the beach for a long walk. Only he hadn't wanted to inconvenience Sarah by suggesting she join him during the still-bad weather. He equally hadn't wished to cut out on her and leave her in the cottage all alone.

"Want to go for a walk?"

"I'd love that. Anything to get some fresh air. How about if we go right after lunch?" He paused a beat. "Only…"

"What?"

"Did you come prepared for rain? Bring any gear?"

She reached over to a side cabinet and lifted a bright red, compact umbrella.

In spite of himself, Matt spurted a laugh. "I meant *real* rain gear. A slicker or something?"

She shook her head, loose tendrils spiraling. Matt recalled the feel of his fingers in her luscious hair as he'd cradled her head in his hands and kissed that glorious mouth. He found himself aching to kiss her again but knew he wouldn't until she was ready.

"Even though the rain's let up, it's still coming down hard enough that I don't think you should go out with *that*. Not with those ocean winds at play. Tell you what," he said with a smile. "Why don't you borrow a slicker of mine? I brought two."

"Two?"

"I like to fish here, and I'm never sure what the weather will be. I learned some time ago it's good to bring a backup supply of clothing. Helps ensure I don't miss any opportunities."

She met his gaze. "That's really nice of you, thanks. I think I'll take you up on it."

By early afternoon they were laughing companionably about the oversized fit of Matt's slicker on Sarah's small frame. "I feel like the Incredible Hulk or something," she said with a giggle. "Something lumbering and large that's about to make its way down the beach. Do you think I'll scare the sand crabs?"

"You're far better looking than the Hulk." Blue eyes crinkled at the corners. "Besides, for the next day or two, I don't think we'll be running into much of anything out there, apart from maybe a few hungry gulls."

Sarah's heart warmed at the thought of spending a few more days in Matt's company. She'd never felt so comfortable around a man. He was alluring and attractive but had never once used his charms to try to seduce her. Instead, he'd played the perfect gentleman, keeping his distance just enough to drive her wild.

"Shall we bring the umbrella?" she asked as they headed for the door.

"Only if you want to watch it flip inside out and risk lifting off into the sky like Mary Poppins."

She grinned and tossed the umbrella across the room and onto the sofa. Sarah recalled a lot of Christmas Eves but certainly couldn't remember any of them being like this. Despite the gloomy weather, this one was off to a great start.

Matt offered Sarah a hand as she made her way down the slick steps. She settled her glove in his grip, the wind whipping her hair wildly about her face. Hers was the face of a Madonna, tinged pink from the nip in the air, her dark eyes warming him even in spite of the chill. He was glad he'd encouraged her to layer up. Thanks to the cold front that had rolled in, temperatures were now in the thirties, icy rain pinging against them like tiny sharp needles. "Are you okay?" he asked with concern. "If it's too rough for you, we can turn back."

She stepped off the last wooden stair, releasing his hand. "Not on your life," she said as the winds blew. He loved that she was feisty, undaunted by the challenge. Some girls might have whimpered and begged to hole up by the fire. Not Sarah in her puffed out Incredible Hulk outfit, he thought with a smile. "Then you might want to tighten your hood a bit to keep your hair from getting wet."

She nodded and fumbled with drawstrings but couldn't seem to work them in her gloves. Matt hadn't worn any. Then again, he was a lot more toughened to the elements than Sarah.

"Here, let me do that," he said, reaching forward to adjust them until they fit right. "Perfect," he said, patting her shoulder. "Ready to roll?"

"I think I'm ready to run!" she said, her teeth chattering slightly. "Standing still lets the damp sink in."

Matt twisted his lips in a smile. "You want to run down the beach through the rain?"

"No," she said, her dark eyes daring. "I want you to see if you can catch me."

Before he knew it, she'd taken off, dashing way ahead of him. Matt chuckled, racing after her, trailing her as she tore along the beach beside the crashing waves. He was closing in and she knew it, giggling like a kid trying to keep her distance. But it was useless. In no time at all, he'd reached her and caught her from behind in his arms. "Ha!" he cried with delight. "Think you could get away from me, did you, lassie?"

She laughed out loud, apparently taken with his pirate talk.

He spun her toward him in his arms, the rain coming down in icy prickles all around them.

She looked up at him through the wind and the rain, her eyes a soulful invitation. He'd be damned if he didn't want to kiss her. And he was nearly damned sure that she wanted him too. Nearly, but not one hundred percent. The last thing he wanted to do was have her run away from him again or to tell him to get packing. Matt didn't know why, but he wasn't sure his heart could take that. Just in these few days together, Sarah had gotten to him in a way he didn't believe possible. And, if she could do this much damage after just a few days, he wasn't sure what kind of shape he'd be in at the end of the week. The first time they'd been together, Matt had blown it badly by not following through. If he'd heeded his instincts three years ago, when Sarah had told him to go, he would have asked why and tried to talk it out. Instead, he'd turned like a chastised puppy dog with his tail between his legs and had rushed off, never fully understanding what had gone wrong. Matt wasn't prepared to risk that again. Not with someone like Sarah. Not when just looking in her eyes made his head swim and his pulse race faster.

Sarah stared up at Matt as the elements raged around them. In spite of the storm, she felt sheltered in his arms, as if she'd found her safe harbor. Something about being with Matt felt so right. How she wished this feeling could go on forever. But there were things about her Matt didn't know. A deep secret that would likely alter his opinion of her and cause him to question becoming involved on more than a casual basis.

"Sarah," he said, his lips hovering above hers. "I'm glad that it worked out this way. That the fates, karma, whatever…somehow put us here together."

"I'm glad too."

"Promise me something." He looked deep in her eyes. Sarah's breath caught in her throat. "Promise you won't run away again without giving me a chance, really taking the time to know me."

But she couldn't promise him that. Couldn't promise absolutely. Just look at what had happened in the past. Of course, neither of her former boyfriends had been halfway as terrific as Matt, which made things all the harder. More than anything, she wanted to open her heart up to this new opportunity. But, when push came to shove, would she be able to? "I can promise I'll try," she said, barely breathing the words.

He steadied her chin in his hand. "There's a rainbow after every storm. You just need to believe it."

She nodded still holding his gaze. The next thing she knew, Matt was pulling her close, bringing his mouth to hers in the rain. "Sarah," he said. He kissed her sweetly, first once, then again and again. "My sweet Sarah, all we need is time." How she wished that were true. The trouble was, she didn't know how much time they really had. But instead of saying so, she let him kiss her over and over, until his soft kisses became deeper ones, and her knees melted like butter.

Chapter Six

Later that evening, Matt and Sarah warmed themselves by the fire. They'd come in soaked but happy from their adventures on the beach, and ravenously hungry besides. The prefab frozen lasagna dinner Sarah had prepared actually wasn't bad. Pairing it with the nice Chianti she'd brought proved a plus, and both had totally enjoyed Matt's homemade garlic bread. Now they sat with two goblets of wine, listening to blues music and the haunting melody of the rain.

It was the most romantic Christmas Eve Matt could remember. If only he had a way to do something special for Sarah and make her really feel the spirit of the holiday. "It's too bad we don't have stockings to hang from the mantel."

"We could always hang up our socks," she said with a grin.

"I don't think you want mine anywhere near a heat source. Especially the ones I went fishing in."

She laughed, seeming to guess that was true. "There *is* a washer in this house, you know."

"Yes. I plan to take advantage of it." He clinked his glass to hers. "Tomorrow."

"It's so hard to believe tomorrow's Christmas," she said with a sigh.

Matt shot her a wink. "We'll have to tuck in early so Santa can come."

"Sure," she said, smiling. "Santa and all his reindeer too."

Matt had pondered the problem all evening. Even given the limited resources at his disposal, he had to come up with some sort of gift. Nothing fancy. Just something to show he'd thought of her. The question was what? Matt had a feeling the answer was right at the tips of his fingers, but he couldn't quite grasp it. "If you could have anything in the world you want, what would you ask for?"

"Anything? That leaves the field wide open."

"I suppose it does."

"You first."

"Me?"

"Fair's fair, Matt. I'm not telling if you won't."

He shared a thoughtful gaze. "Well… If I'm being really honest, I guess what I want… We're talking some day…" He held her hand and smiled, sending wild butterflies fluttering inside her. "Is what my parents have. That kind of life." Naturally he would. Theirs was such a lovely example to follow, Sarah thought with a touch of melancholy.

"That makes perfect sense," she said softly.

"Now you," he urged, giving her hand a light squeeze.

She considered this a moment, watching the flames dance and leap in the hearth. After a beat she turned her face to his, her cheeks warm from the fire. "If I really could have anything…"

"*Anything*," he said for emphasis.

"Well," she said truthfully, "I've always wanted to visit Tasmania. See the Southern Cross."

"Tasmania, huh?" he said with surprise. "That's quite a wish!"

She nudged him with her elbow. "You did say *anything*."

"Tasmania's a nice dream. Nothing at all the matter with that." He wrapped his arm around her and tucked her in close. "It's just a little tough to fit under a tree."

"That's the other thing," she said, looking up at him.

"What is?"

"A tree. I've always thought it would be really lovely to have a tree. A real live Christmas tree."

Matt knew she'd said her mom hadn't ever celebrated, but he was a tad surprised she'd never bought a tree of her own. "You've never had one?"

"I did break down and buy a small Christmas tree prism. It hangs from the rearview mirror of my SUV."

"I meant, for your apartment?"

"It hardly seemed practical with no ornaments to put on it."

"You can buy those."

She looked at him sincerely. "That's not the same. Tree ornaments were meant to be homemade."

"And why is that?"

"Because," she said with certainty, "it means they were made with love. And that's really what the season's about in so many ways."

"You never made any yourself?"

She hung her head, averting his gaze. "I'm about as crafty as I am a Betty Crocker."

He chuckled lightly, tightening his embrace around her shoulders. "You're a wonderful Betty Crocker. The best cook I've ever met, in fact."

She slowly met his eyes, the firelight catching in hers. "Honestly?"

"Honey, there's no one I'd rather bake cookies with."

She beamed at him. How he loved it when she smiled. In fact, her smile was quickly becoming one of Matt's favorite things. "Thanks for saying that, even if it's not true."

"But it is true," he protested with a laugh. It was too. There was no other woman he wanted in his arms when giving instructions on the rolling pin.

"In any case," she continued, "I'm sure I'll get one someday. A Christmas tree, I mean. I'd really like to, anyhow."

Matt held her close, the most brilliant idea occurring. It wouldn't be exact, but it might work well enough. If only he could find that box Robert kept below the house.

A little while later, Matt had kissed her sweetly and said they should rest up for Christmas Day. Sarah went to bed, but her restless emotions had kept her tossing and turning for hours. On one hand, she was elated that a man as incredible as Matt would take an interest in her. He was dynamite to be around and every bit the fantastic kisser she'd remembered. Conversely, she felt down knowing what she kept from him. Could she really hope he'd still want to see her if he knew the truth? Sarah still wasn't done dealing with it, and it had caused her untold hours of anguish. She hadn't even dared to tell her best friend. Somehow, by sharing bad news, you made it that much more real. As long as she dealt with this alone, she could handle it. Then again, handling things alone meant that *alone* was how she'd always be.

Sarah rolled onto her side and hugged her pillow, a tear sliding down her cheek. In the soft glow of the nightlight, she could make out the contours of her room and its huge windows framing the sea. Though she couldn't view it due to the darkness, she could still hear the pounding of the waves against the shore. The rain must have let up; before, its fierce ruckus had overtaken the ocean's roar.

Sarah sat up under the covers, thinking she'd heard the screen door creak open. But how could that be? She studied the clock on the nightstand. It was nearly four a.m. She slid into her slippers, determined to check, and hoping that Matt had heard it too. Even if it had just been the wind knocking the screen door ajar, she'd feel much safer checking it with big, strapping Matt around. Spying her cell on the dresser, she got an idea. She'd call Matt and ask if he'd heard something too. No, that was silly. She couldn't possibly wake him for an unlikely reason. For all intents and purposes, they were marooned on this island together. Who knew how close their nearest neighbor was? She'd initially assumed the house next door was occupied, but as it turned out, that high-end hybrid SUV that had been parked in the drive belonged to Matt. It probably *was* just the wind, Sarah told herself, trying to settle back down. She sat on the bed, but a split second later heard the same noise again. She sprang to her feet, grabbing the nearest weapon she could find, her bright red umbrella. With a shaky hand, she opened the door to the living area, hoping to goodness this was all in her mind. Surely she'd check the house and find everything clear. Otherwise, she aimed to beeline it into Matt's room just as quickly as she could, propriety be damned.

The second she stepped over the threshold, a bright beam of light pierced her vision.

"Sarah!" Matt called from the doorway, steadying his flashlight in her direction.

"Matt!" she cried, equally in shock. "What are you doing?" He wore a damp rain slicker and appeared to be carting some sort of box indoors.

He set down the box and lowered the beam of his flashlight. When he spoke again, he sounded slightly out of breath. "Fishing."

"Fishing?"

"Yeah, I..." He smiled tightly. "Though you'd appreciate a nice Christmas dinner. Catch of the Day?" he said with a shrug.

Sarah thought something smelled fishy, all right. Since when did people catch fish at four a.m.? And who in their right mind would pack them in cardboard?

He stared at the umbrella angled high in her hand. "Where were you going with *that*?"

"To beat the living daylights out of whoever was breaking in here."

"What if it had been Santa? Since when have you taken to clubbing geriatric citizens?"

Sarah lowered the umbrella and narrowed her gaze. "Hmm, yes," she said, growing suspicious. "What's in the box?"

Matt scratched his head, his eyes darting toward the door, then back toward hers again. "Can't say."

"Can't or won't?"

"Can't/won't. There's a slash in there."

"Matt..." she began. "I'm sure you weren't fishing."

"Got me there," he said brightly. "Doesn't mean I'm not about to!"

"You mean you're going down on the beach now?"

"Down on the beach. Into the waves. Knee-deep if I have to. Yup."

"Then what?"

"Then, I'm headed straight back up here and hitting the hay. Precisely as you ought to." He went about his work as he spoke, hoisting the mysterious box and sliding it into his bedroom, then reemerging with a tackle box and his fishing pole and its holder. My, he was acting strange. Odder than she'd ever seen him.

"Are you sure you should be fishing at this hour?"

"Sarah, I'm a man of the wild. Nature and I? We're like this." He set down his gear to lace his hands together in a tug. "Why don't you go back to bed? I'll be back before long and will see you in the morning."

"All right. If you're sure?"

"Megapositive," he said, picking up his gear and flashing her a grin.

Matt left his gear under the house, then headed for the beach, the beam of his flashlight leading. Whew! That had been close. He wasn't sure whether Sarah had believed his fishing story, but one way or another, he was confident things would come out fine. Now, if he could just locate that huge piece of driftwood he'd spotted when he and Sarah had been here earlier today…

Matt trudged through the sludgy sand, his heart light. So yeah, the beach roads were crappy. Impassable, in fact. In many ways, that was the best Christmas gift he'd ever had. Out of the blue, life had delivered him a second chance with Sarah. A woman from his past who could very well become a permanent fixture in his future. Sarah was beautiful and funny and kind, just the sort of person he'd always imagined himself winding up with. Him and a big bustling passel of kids.

Matt stopped walking, shocked at his own thoughts. Had he just considered making babies with Sarah? Yeah, he had, he thought, feeling his lips tug into a broad grin. Not that he was accustomed to getting ahead of himself, but Matt couldn't help but wonder what that might be like. Just him and Sarah—and their big happy brood— all adorning the family Christmas tree with homemade decorations. Matt recalled how much fun it had been sitting around the kitchen table, making those crafts with his sisters and brother Robert. He'd even enjoyed working with his nieces last Christmas when they'd taught him how to fashion Christmas stars from pieces of tinfoil with little holes poked in them to let through the light. While he didn't have ornament hooks from which to hang them, he had fishing wire to use as a handy substitution. Yes sir, his plan was going to work out fine. All he had to hope was that the tide hadn't washed out his special surprise.

Chapter Seven

Sarah awakened early and stretched in bed. She didn't know what had caused her to rise before seven o'clock. Generally, she slept until eight. Then suddenly she remembered. Of course! Today was Christmas Day! But what did that matter, really? How much could she expect at a beach house on the rugged North Carolina coast? She'd never partaken much in Christmas, anyway. And here she was, stuck with a man who'd never even expected her to be here. And was much less prepared to make the holiday special for her, besides. Sarah unfolded the simple poem she'd composed for Matt, hoping it wasn't desperately inane. All she'd longed to do was give him something of her heart. She'd wanted to say thank you and had thought for a brief moment that this was a good way to start. Now, looking down at her uneven scrawl, she doubted her instincts. What if he thought her a fool, or worse yet—questioned her iambic pentameter? Sarah's poetry had never been in perfect rhythm, but at least it was concise and summarized what she wanted to say.

After Matt had sent her to bed, she'd stayed up an extra hour trying hard to fashion its lines. He'd been so kind, and all she meant to say was thank you. *Thanks for being the kind of guy I'd always believed was in this world.* Since Sarah had been a little girl, she'd been putting words together. Sometimes clumsily; at others, in a neatly arrayed fashion. Her English teachers had told her she had talent, though she'd refused in many ways to believe it. What was important to her more than anything was reaching the people she felt driven to write for. Since coming here, Matt had become one of those people.

Sarah folded over the page, deciding that she'd have to give it to him. Most especially because what they had might not last. And, in the end, she thought with a heavy heart, it was destined not to.

Matt put on the finishing touches, feeling exhausted. He'd work hard all night to ensure everything would come off right. Since he was committed to protecting the environment, he hadn't been about to insult a flourishing pine. Instead, he'd selected found driftwood as the perfect stand-in "Charlie Brown" yuletide tree. With the summer deck lights strung around it, it looked almost festive. The tinfoil ornaments he'd fashioned thanks to his nieces' help had been a boon. Just last season, he'd sat with the three little girls around his mom's kitchen table. They'd taught him a trick they'd learned in Brownie Scouts. How to create shiny star ornaments from cutout pieces of aluminum foil, dotted with pinprick holes to let through the light. They were somewhat reminiscent of Mexican lanterns, only hung from the branches of this wayward tree. Matt felt lucky that, in lieu of ornament hooks, he'd had fishing wire with which to secure them. He hoped with all his heart that Sarah would enjoy it. It certainly looked regal enough, standing nearly five feet tall and spreading its spindling braches wide on all sides.

Matt thought he heard stirring from Sarah's room and debated whether to flee or to stay and wish her a merry Christmas. Before he'd fully processed that thought, she opened her bedroom door and suddenly appeared.

"Oh my." She brought her palms to her perfectly pink cheeks. "What's this?"

"Merry Christmas," he said, his tone husky.

She stopped in her tracks and met his gaze, her voice wavering. "Is this what I think it is?"

He turned to her, his heart pounding. Of all the mornings he'd ever experienced, this was the one he hoped would go off right. "Your very own Christmas tree."

She approached it slowly, then gingerly touched one of its branches. "Driftwood?" she asked, amazement in her eyes.

"I had to get creative," he answered honestly.

"Oh, Matt," she said, her voice cracking. She'd never had anyone do something like this for her before. How he'd done it or where he'd found the lights and decorations, she had no idea. But one thing was clear, the look in his eyes said he'd done it all for her. So this was what he'd been up to late last night with that box and why he'd snuck down on the beach. She gingerly touched one of the stars, and it pivoted on its thin wire, tiny arrays of light streaking through its pattern of holes. "Did you make this?"

He smiled, and the tears that had been aching to break through poured from her eyes. "I can't believe you did this... Did this all for me."

"I wanted to do something for you. Something to show you you're special."

How she wanted to show him he was special too. Sarah debated about giving him the poem but decided to put it off until later. She wasn't sure how he might take it, and, given how well things were going now, she didn't want to put a damper on them. "Thank you. It's wonderful. Probably the most wonderful Christmas gift I've ever received."

He took her in his arms. "I was hoping to make this day great for you."

"It couldn't be any more perfect," she said, looking up in his eyes. And it was true. Sarah was feeling so bright and hopeful this morning. So positive, in fact, that she didn't want any sort of negativity to get in the way. Ever since that first late-night conversation with Matt, she'd struggled with her attraction to him and been conflicted about becoming involved. But he was so warm and wonderful, it was hard not to be tempted to let those doubts slide. Just once, Sarah wanted to feel good about things and bask in this dynamite man's attentions. Would it really be so wrong for them to have one ideal day where she could let herself go and live in the moment?

Matt glanced sideways, then sexily cocked an eyebrow. "Not even…if it's snowing?"

She stared in delight out the large glass door to see a billion little white flakes driving down in droves to coat the deck framing the ocean. The scene was lovely, magical in its unexpected beauty. Matt took her hand and led her toward the door. "Come on!"

"We can't go out there like this!" she said, referring to their sleeping attire.

"You're right." He nabbed a throw blanket from the sofa. "We'll use this to keep us warm."

But when he led her outdoors, Sarah realized she wouldn't need the blanket at all. Matt scooped her in his arms, wrapping the blanket around them as snow beat down on the deck. She looked up at him as a smile worked its way across his handsome face. "There really is a Santa," she said. Snow drove down harder, coating their hair with tiny white flakes. He brushed his lips to hers, and her world went all warm and fuzzy, in spite of the freezing cold. "I'm looking at him."

"You're all I want for Christmas. I'm so happy you're here."

He kissed her harder then, his deep passion sweeping her away while the wind and the snow swirled around them and the pounding ocean echoed the rhythm of their hearts.

A little while later, they sat wrapped up in a fresh blanket on the sofa before a cozy fire, both sipping from mugs of hot cocoa. "I've never had a holiday like this," she told Matt honestly. "This one's been like a dream."

"And it's not over yet." He gave her shoulder a tight hug. "I was thinking of making us some gumbo for Christmas dinner. How does that sound?"

"Delicious. Do you have everything you need?"

"Catch of the Day," he said with a grin.

Sarah gasped at his revelation. "Are you saying you really went fishing last night?"

"It was more like early this morning, but yeah."

"I thought you were sneaking outdoors, preparing all this." She motioned to the makeshift Christmas tree beside them, sharing its homey glow.

"I was," he told her. "But once I'd set the driftwood under the house to dry out a bit, I came back and got my fishing gear. You'll really like the gumbo, I think. It's not exactly turkey and stuffing, but—"

"It sounds great. Just let me know what I can do to help."

He wriggled his eyebrows. "Are you making a play to start cooking with me again?"

She laughed. "Might be."

"You won't have to offer twice." He smiled softly. "Though I've got to admit making a roux won't be nearly as sexy as baking cookies."

Her lips took a downward turn. "Darn."

He took her hand in his. "How did I get so lucky? One day I'm all over women, and the next, there you are."

"All over women?"

"It doesn't matter, really. I'm just happy my brother insisted I come here to get away."

"So it was Robert's idea, was it?"

"Uh-huh. Was it yours or Elaine's?"

"Elaine's, actually."

He gave a hearty laugh. "Well, God bless them both. We'll have to drink a toast to them later."

Sarah had fun helping Matt with the gumbo. Though he'd been right, making a roux wasn't nearly as sexy as baking cookies. It required devoted attention to hot oil and flour, and careful timing with tossing in chopped onions and celery. After a delicious dinner filled with easy conversation and laughter, Sarah helped Matt with the cleanup, which was minimal.

"What would you like to do now?" he asked her. "Shall we look for a movie?"

But Sarah was having so much fun talking with Matt, she didn't want to find them caught up in something like that. "Maybe we could turn on some music and just visit awhile?"

"Sounds great to me." He went to the living area to survey the CDs, neatly alphabetized on some built-in shelves. "What will it be? Christmas music or the Beach Boys?"

"Hmm. Tough decision. Why don't we go with Beach Boys. I mean, given where we are."

He grinned and loaded the CD. When *Little St. Nick* began to play, Sarah laughed. "Looks like we're getting both! The Beach Boys *and* Christmas."

"At least with this song," he said with a chuckle.

She carried her wine to the sofa, but before she could get there, Matt approached.

"Care to dance?"

"Sure," she said, setting her glass aside. The music was catchy and upbeat as he took her in his arms and they bounced happily to its tune. He twirled her under his arm, then whirled her back toward him, tucking her up against him. She laughed heartily. "Where did you learn to dance like this?"

"In North Carolina, they call this shag dancing. It's big in the beach areas."

When the song ended, a slower one started. Sarah turned to head back to the sofa, but Matt stopped her by taking her hand.

"Don't go."

She gazed up at him, and blue eyes sparkled, warm in the firelight's glow. "I need you to stay with me," he said, his voice gone husky, as *Don't Worry, Baby* began. "Stay in my arms."

He pulled her to him, and they embraced her pulse fluttering wildly. "This is all I want," he whispered into her hair as he held her close. "Just to be with you. Right here and now."

It was all she wanted too. Everything she wanted and had always longed for was right here in front of her. Sarah held on tight as they swayed to the music and the embers of the fire crackled softly. When the brief snow shower had let up, a deep fog had moved in. From faraway on the sound, the mournful cry of a tugboat wafted across the waters. They'd been through all kinds of weather, but with Matt, she'd felt safe, secure in the knowledge that he would care for and comfort her.

She would remember this Christmas forever.

Chapter Eight

The next morning, they sat at the kitchen island with their coffees.

"I can't believe we got a white Christmas," she said. "I can't remember the last time I had one. I had to have been a kid."

"A light dusting was more like it," he said with a laugh. "But, you're right. It was special."

She studied him with affection, thinking how much she'd come to care for him these past few days. No matter what happened later, she would always recall her time here with him in a fond way. "I want to thank you. Thank you for helping make yesterday the best Christmas ever." She shifted in her seat to pull the poem from her jeans pocket. She'd debated about giving it to him at all but then had decided she needed to let him know that she'd thought of him.

She handed it over, apologizing. "I considered giving this to you yesterday but decided to wait. I hope you don't mind."

"Of course I don't mind." He appeared genuinely touched by the gesture.

He unfolded the page and looked down at the carefully crafted lines. "This is wonderful," he said, meeting her gaze. "I've never had anyone do anything like this for me before."

"I've never had anyone make me a Christmas tree out of driftwood."

He smiled at her warmly, then lowered his head and began to read.

Between the earth and sky,
You and I
Are caught up
In this moment,
Where waves crash,
And lightning strikes
The shore.
You're deep
In my soul,
Warming
The cold
Of my heart.

After a lingering moment, he looked up. "It's beautiful," he said, the words catching in his throat. "But also a little sad, don't you think?"

"I thought it was hopeful."

"Then I'll take it as that way too." He stared through the plate glass door, studying the horizon. "Looks like the storm has lifted. How about you and I take a stroll?"

Matt led her onto the beach, where soft winds blew and gulls called. The sky was cloudy yet calm, the ocean roiling peacefully below it. They walked a long way down the shore, neither one talking. There was an unspoken melancholy between them, as if each sensed their time together was drawing to a close.

"I want to thank you for the poem," he said finally. "It means a lot to me that you'd write it."

"It was nothing."

He stopped walking to look at her. "No, it was something. Something really beautiful that came from your heart."

Sarah felt herself flush. Oh, how she wished she could give him that heart, wholly and unconditionally. But there'd been conditions imposed on her she couldn't help or change.

Matt took her gently by the shoulders and gazed in her eyes. "But Sarah, I want… Need you to understand. This is more than a *brief moment* for me. I mean, I want it to be more than that for both of us."

Emotion swirled within her. "Just what are you saying?"

"That I don't believe we both wound up here by accident. That maybe there was something else at play. Something bigger than the two of us, and maybe even more magical than…Santa."

"It's been really wonderful, but—"

"I'm not talking about anything drastic. Rather that we take this incredible serendipity as some sort of sign. A sign that maybe we weren't meant to walk away from each other three years ago. Then again, maybe we were, because things can be that much better between us now.

"All I'm asking is that when the ferry reopens, things between us won't end. Let me take you out to dinner back in Bethesda. Maybe even a movie. We don't have to rush things. There's nothing wrong with taking our time."

She pressed her lips together for a beat, studying him. When she finally spoke, her chin trembled. "I can't give you what you want."

"You don't even *know* what I want," he said, his voice etched with pain.

Sarah dropped her eyes to hide the fact that they were watering.

"I'm not the girl for you. Not long-term."

"Is it…" he began tentatively, appearing stung by the thought. "Is it that you don't feel the same way?"

"It doesn't matter how I feel."

"Sarah, please. Talk to me."

She gathered her resolve and met his eyes, knowing this was for the best. Sometimes when you really cared for someone, you had to do what was right for that person. Not selfishly only consider yourself. Matt deserved to have the sort of life he was destined to lead. And that life couldn't include her.

"I'm not interested. Not interested in any more than we've had here."

Matt sucked in a breath and stared at her in disbelief.

"I guess that's all I needed to hear," he said hoarsely.

The telephone rang loudly as they reentered the house from their walk. Matt walked in a daze to answer it. So she didn't feel the same. Had no interest in continuing things further. He'd done nothing more than make one big fool of himself his whole time here. He lifted the receiver with a heavy heart as gulls sailed beyond the kitchen window. "Hello?"

It was the ferryman, advising all residents on the island that the boat docks were nearly repaired. With the bad weather ended, the ferry would be up and running again the first thing tomorrow. Well, that was something, anyway. He and Sarah would no longer be trapped here together. Given the conversation they'd just had, that was obviously for the best.

"Who was that?" she asked from the living area.

"The ferry will back in business tomorrow. I guess I should start packing."

"No, don't," she said suddenly. "You can stay. I'll go."

And, for the first time since she'd arrived here, Matt didn't feel any inclination to stop her.

The next day, Matt sat at the table, watching the waves through the window. The skies had mostly cleared, except for a few dark clouds rumbling above. Scattered showers were predicted, but there were heavier rains raging inside him. He felt all turned inside out, as if someone had extracted his heart and laid it on this very table. And someone had. Her name was Sarah.

"I'm leaving," she said, standing by the kitchen door.

Matt glanced her way and set down his coffee. She'd already loaded her SUV and now held nothing but her small purse and a travel water bottle. "I see."

"Matt…" Her cheeks were flushed. "If there was any way to work things out, I'd stay." Like hell she would. She hadn't even given them a chance, wouldn't even tell him what was wrong. She was just playing herself again, calling the shots, and getting to be the one who decided when it was over. "You're going to miss the boat."

She sucked in a breath, and it sounded like she was crying. Matt didn't dare turn to look at her. He studied the shore instead, watching it take a relentless beating from the waves. His heart knew just how that felt.

He heard the door creak open as she spoke, her voice shaky. "It was good seeing you again."

In a different world, he might have felt the same. At the moment, though, all Matt wanted was for her to go away so that the pain would end.

Chapter Nine

Sarah waited in line for the ferry, queued up behind two other SUVs and a couple of pickups. These were the greatest signs of life she'd seen in days, and still they were paltry. Few folks ventured to the island this time of year, and those who did were die-hards. Rugged outdoorsmen or property owners, the types not easily put off by a ten-foot storm surge or the occasional nor'easter. She peered through her windshield at the darkening sky. More bad weather was coming, but it could nowhere compete with the storm in her soul. Her parting from Matt had been heartbreaking, yet necessary. Wasn't it so much better to say good-bye now, when becoming even more involved would only make separating worse? He'd told her just what he wanted: the same thing his parents had. She knew what that was because she'd seen it firsthand. A warm, wonderful family with lots of offspring, and having children was not in Sarah's future.

She steeled her heart, worried that she'd always be alone. After rupturing her appendix in college, she'd developed pelvic inflammatory disease, a horrible infection. Its outcome had left her sterile, completely unable to bear children. It was a bitter pill to swallow at age twenty-one and apparently had been too much for her college boyfriend to deal with. They'd talked about graduating and moving to work in the same city. Eventually getting married and raising a family of their own. While he hadn't left her immediately, receiving news of her medical condition had seemed to change the way he felt about her. Though he denied it, afterward things started breaking apart. They began fighting more frequently, then finally split up the second semester of their senior year.

Later, Sarah had chalked up her college boyfriend's reaction to youth and inexperience. Surely a mature man who loved her deeply wouldn't react the same way. She'd learned differently with her first adult relationship in Maryland. It wasn't that he hadn't loved her; it was more that he'd seen a different sort of future for them going forward. Naturally, adoption was an option, but he'd been the only son in his family and had always thought he'd carry on the family line. When he'd also gone away, the breakup had ripped Sarah's heart to shreds with its haunting déjà vu. Consequently, it had become harder for her to become intimate with a man. She'd surprised herself by falling into bed with Matt at Elaine's wedding.

Now that she knew the truth, she could more clearly piece together what had happened. She'd not only been desperately attracted to him, she'd also seen him as someone with potential. Serious potential. He was intelligent, witty, and unbearably handsome, just the sort of guy she'd always known she'd fall for. The more champagne she'd had, the better he'd looked. And the better he'd looked, the more devastated she was by her secret. Here he was, this super terrific guy, and their mutual attraction was powerful. So powerful, Sarah wasn't sure if she could fight it. Part of her wanted to totally give in, see if things would follow through and they might begin a relationship. But most of her was utterly terrified that what had happened in the past would occur again. In her fits and starts between wanting him and wanting to flee from him in order to protect her still fragile heart, she'd drunk herself silly.

If only she'd believed it wouldn't have made a difference to Matt, she would have told him the truth. But he was so clearly into his family and the concept of a big, happy brood. After spending time with him this week at the beach, she believed that more than ever. His background was not just Italian but also Catholic. Sarah recalled all the toasts and jokes that were made at Elaine and Robert's wedding about making tons of babies, and quickly. Creating lots of little Salvatores was clearly a family expectation, one that she'd be unable to fulfill.

Needing to distract herself from her pain, Sarah switched on her satellite radio. It was set to a blues station, and the song *Stormy Weather* began to play. As if on cue, light rain began to ping against the windshield, flecking it with little dots of moisture that ran in sad streaks down the glass. She shut her eyes as Etta James crooned on, and the memories from the week flooded back. Catching Matt by surprise as he emerged in a towel from the outdoor shower... Enjoying movies and board games together... Matt wrapping his arms around her during that very sexy baking lesson... Kissing him in the rain and in the snow... And finally, that truly magical Christmas tree he'd so lovingly crafted for her on Christmas morning morning.

A horn blared, and Sarah opened her eyes to see the queue ahead of her was moving, the ferryman motioning vehicles onto the broad deck of the boat. She wiped her tears with her coat sleeve and set her vehicle in gear, her hands trembling. Despite the damp cold, her heart was on fire, burning like a forest blaze consuming its final pine. There was nothing much left of her; she had nothing left to give. Why, then, had Matt seemed to trust that she did? Sarah rolled onto the ferry, her SUV rising and falling over the loading ramp with a jolt, as Etta James begged to see the sun... Just then, a beam of sunlight streaked in through her windshield from behind a faraway cloud.

The Christmas-tree-shaped crystal dangling from Sarah's rearview mirror pivoted in its glow, dazzling her with an astounding array of color. Matt's words came back to her in a husky whisper. *"There's a rainbow after every storm,"* he'd said, looking into her eyes. *"You just need to believe it."*

Sarah's heart beat faster as she knew suddenly what she must do. She could no longer run from her life. She had to confront it head-on. She needed to start by gathering her courage to explain things to Matt. Even if he didn't want her after what she had to say, he deserved to hear the truth. He'd been nothing but good and kind to her. So thoughtful and romantic too. It was wrong of her to leave without any explanation at all, leaving him to wonder if he'd somehow been at fault. How could she do that to someone as great as him when the blame was hers and hers alone? It was time for her to stand up and own it, letting the cards fall where they may. But oh, didn't her heart hope that would land her in Matt's arms.

She glanced in her rearview mirror and gasped. Another car was getting loaded onto the ferry behind her. Then another...and yet another still. "Wait!" she shouted, throwing up her hands. The ferryman continued his work, unable to hear her. She couldn't let this happen. Not here, not today. The year was coming to an end, so maybe it was time to consider new beginnings. Sarah laid on her horn and opened her driver's side door, leaping from the SUV. "Stop!" she yelled at the stunned ferryman, who stared at her beneath his tartan-plaid tam. "Off! I've got to get off," she continued, a bit breathless. "Off of this boat!"

"I'm afraid that's impossible, lady. We're already halfway loaded."

Sarah glanced at the line of nearly a dozen vehicles behind her, then met the ferryman's gaze. "What if I ask them all to back up?"

"What?"

"I'll do it! I'll go car to car if I have to!"

"What is this? Some sort of emergency?"

It most certainly was. In fact, it was the greatest state of emergency Sarah Anderson had ever had. For the first time in her life, she was falling for the perfect man, *a good man, a wonderful man,* and she was being foolish enough to let him get away. It was time she learned to fight for her life, work for the future she wanted. Even if it proved painful. Even if she might fail. The hard truth was she'd never forgive herself if she didn't try. "Yes."

The ferryman removed his tam and slowly shook his head before looking up. "What kind of an emergency?"

"It's..." Sarah felt her voice warble and pursed her lips a beat to steady herself. "...my heart."

His faced creased with concern, and he took a step forward. She held up a hand to stop him.

"Two hearts, really. There's a very big risk of someone getting hurt. Of both hearts being broken."

The ferryman heaved a sigh, his expression lighting with understanding. "And you think that by getting off this boat, you can fix it?"

She stared at him, feeling her confidence surge. "I have to try."

Back at the cottage, Matt morosely disassembled his makeshift Christmas tree. Sarah had looked just like some delighted kid when she'd happened upon it Christmas morning. He'd really thought he'd done everything right, but apparently his efforts had been a major fail. What a fiasco this trip had been. He'd come to beach to forget about one woman and had been unexpectedly raked over the coals by another one. Maybe what Matt needed to do was take a break from women altogether. A long break.

He was just coiling up the deck lights when he thought he heard a car in the drive, screeching to a halt. Seconds later, a door popped open, then slammed shut. Could that be Sarah? Coming back to retrieve something she'd forgotten?

His answer came in the sound of her footfalls racing up the front steps. "Matt!" she said, bursting through the kitchen door. "We have to talk!" She was out of breath, her coat unzipped and her sweatshirt and hair speckled by the light rain that had been falling.

"I thought you were catching the ferry?"

"I was," she said, stepping forward and shutting the door behind her. "But I got off."

"Off?" he questioned, trying to imagine that feat, particularly if she'd already been loaded. "Sarah, what's going on?"

She crossed to where he stood, and looked up, her brown eyes brimming with moisture. "I haven't been completely honest. There's something. Something that I need to tell you."

Matt swallowed hard, not knowing what to expect. "And what is that?"

"I can't…" She stopped, seeming to gather her nerve.

"Are you changing your mind? About the two of us?"

"I've never wanted anything but the two of us."

"Then why…?"

"I can't have children," she said in a whimper. "A long time ago, I had an infection, and—"

He brought his fingers to her lips. "Is that why you left? Why you said we couldn't have a future? Because you believed that was a deal breaker for me?"

She held his gaze through bleary eyes. "Isn't it?"

While he'd never had occasion to consider it, the truth was he wasn't about to let someone as amazing as Sarah get away due to a medical condition beyond her control. What kind of man would that make him? Not the one he understood himself to be. It must have taken tremendous courage for Sarah to come back and tell him the truth, particularly as she had no guarantee what his reaction might be. "No. It isn't," he said, knowing when he said it that answer felt right.

"But you said… You told me that you want what your parents have."

"I meant *their relationship*. The way they are with each other and are there for one another, even after all these years." He took her in his arms, damp clothing and all. "Sweetheart, listen to me. I want *you*. Do you hear me? You're the person I'm falling in love with and can't bear to see walk away. Please promise me you won't do that again. Twice was bad enough. I'm not sure my heart can take a third time."

She shared a shaky smile, tears streaming from her eyes. "I promise."

"Besides…" He lightly stroked her cheeks. "Some say that kids are overrated."

"They do not," she said with a sniff. "Especially in your family."

"There are options, you know. Life is full of options." He grinned warmly. "I like dogs."

She laughed through her tears. "You're such a great guy."

"Hmm, yes. I'm glad you can finally see that. Only from this point out, I'm going to insist on one thing." He pressed his forehead to hers and looked deeply in her eyes. "That you call me Santa."

"What?" she asked with surprise.

"I thought it was kind of sexy when you said I was like him."

"You *are* him," she said, tugging him close.

He threaded his fingers in her luscious hair and drew her in for a kiss. After an intensely passionate moment, he pulled back. "Can I convince you to stay for New Year's?"

"Why, Santa," she said softly, "we don't even have champagne."

He laughed out loud, snuggling her in his arms. "We'll improvise."

He kissed her deeply then, again and again, only finding himself hungry for more. She molded herself to him, her legs appearing to give way. But he shored her up and held her close, determined now—more than ever—never to let her go.

Epilogue

The following December, Matt took Sarah's hand and led her onto the big, broad deck. The ocean bellowed and tumbled before them, gulls darting in and out of the waves under a darkening sky. Matt wrapped his arms around her from behind as they studied the seascape.

"Looks like a storm's brewing."

She glanced over her shoulder thinking he was the most handsome man she'd seen in *anything*—a tuxedo or a towel. "Hmm, yes. We could be stuck here indefinitely."

"Now, that would be a shame." He leaned forward and nuzzled her neck, causing her to shiver slightly.

"Chilly?"

The wind kicked up ruffling the layers of her billowy white gown. "Just a bit."

Matt removed his jacket and draped it over her shoulders before turning her toward him in an embrace. "I'm glad we bought this place."

"I couldn't think of a better spot to spend our honeymoon," she said, smiling up at him.

He shot her a sexy grin. "And this time we brought champagne."

"What will we toast to?"

Her face warmed under his perusal. "Santa?"

"Yes. To him and Christmastime."

Matt brushed his lips to hers. "Spending Christmas with you is the best."

"Something tells me it's about to get even better," she said, nearly breathless.

"Shall I carry you back to the sleigh?"

"I'll go anywhere with you," she said, meaning it absolutely.

"How about a trip around the world?"

"*What?*"

"You did say you wanted to see the Southern Cross? Travel to Tasmania?"

"You can't mean…?".

"Sarah, sweetheart," he said with a loving look. "I've arranged some time off, and we've got plenty of money."

"But I thought this was our honeymoon?"

"Beach baby of mine, *the honeymoon* has just begun."

The End

A Note from the Author

Thanks for reading *Beach Blanket Santa*. I hope you enjoyed it. If you did, please help other people find this book.

1. This book is lendable, so loan it to a friend who you think might like it so that she (or he) can discover me, too.

2. Help other people find this book: write a review.

3. Sign up for my newsletter so that that you can learn about the next book as soon as it's available. Write to GinnyBairdRomance@gmail.com with "newsletter" in the subject heading.

4. Come like my Facebook page: http://www.facebook.com/GinnyBairdRomance.

5. Comment on my blog: The Story Behind the Story at http://www.goodreads.com.

6. Visit my website: http://www.ginnybairdromance.com for details on other books available at multiple outlets now.

Printed in Great Britain
by Amazon